NIGHTWAVES

NIGHTWAVES

Scary Tales for After Dark

COLLIN McDONALD

COBBLEHILL BOOKS

Dutton   New York

Library of Congress Cataloging-in-Publication Data
McDonald, Collin, date
Nightwaves : scary tales for after dark / Collin McDonald.
p.   cm.
Summary: A collection of horror stories featuring a spirit hunter
from ancient Egypt, two ghosts at a dangerous dam, a woman who
sells her husband's soul to the devil, and a mad killer
in the woods.
ISBN 0-525-65043-1
1. Horror tales, American.   [1. Horror stories.   2. Supernatural—
Fiction.   3. Short stories.]   I. Title.
PZ7.M4784176Ni   1990   [Fic]—dc20
90-35234   CIP   AC

Published in the United States by Cobblehill Books,
an affiliate of Dutton Children's Books,
a division of Penguin Books USA Inc.

Designed by Jean Krulis
Printed in the United States of America
First Edition   10 9 8 7 6 5 4 3 2 1

To Dawn, to Dad and Mom and to Gramp,
of course;
and especially to Scott and Brandon,
now nearly grown,
whose repeated requests long ago
to "please tell us a story"
were the genesis of the present collection.

CONTENTS

GERANIUMS 9

THE VISIT OF JOSHUA SOMETHING 22

THE RADIO 34

THE DAM 46

THE MUSIC TEACHER 58

COLOR CRAZY 75

FOREST EYES 87

CHANGING BURT 102

GERANIUMS

In spite of herself, Janet looked forward to the spring of the year with a growing sense of excitement. School was almost over, and the cold, gray chill of winter was giving way once again to buttery warm sunshine. Green grass was peeking again through the crust of winter-hardened ground. Tiny leaf buds, like cheerful visitors, were beginning to pop out on the elm and maple trees around her house.

Each year Janet hoped that this spring would be different, that it would bring a change from all the other springs. And each year nothing changed. Each year, her mother made her help with the planting. She would have to go with her mother to the large garden plot behind their house and start to get the soil ready for the seeds. Later she would have to go along to the store, where her mother would select seeds and bulbs for this year's display.

While her friends were getting ready for summer camp and going to the beach and planning cookouts, Janet would be on her knees on the damp ground, getting blisters and thorn pricks on her hands and planting more seeds. To Janet's mother it was impossible to plant too many flowers or have too large a garden.

Whenever Janet asked if she could have a cookout or go to camp sometime, her mother always said the same thing:

"You're all I have, dear," she would say, sometimes bringing a frail, tired sound to her voice. "Since your father left us, we have only each other, and the flowers."

In fact, Janet felt like running away. And the truth was, she *hated* flowers.

"I *hate* you," she would whisper to the roses, even as she packed more soil carefully around the base of each bush. "And I *really* hate your stupid thorns." To the lilies, she would sneer secretly, so her mother couldn't see, and sometimes she stuck her tongue out at the pansies.

No matter how much she hated the garden, each year it grew larger with more geraniums, marigolds, daisies, tulips, and roses.

"I hope you dry up and *die!*" Janet whispered to the petals, vines, and bushes as she passed.

Lots of people plant vegetables in their gardens, thought Janet, but my mom likes only flowers—rows and rows of them, everywhere there's a space. Each year her mother reserved more of their land for the garden, until they had almost no backyard at all, and each year they added flowers. Each year the garden crept outward, with leaf petals from one fence line to the other.

The neighbors around Janet's house had known about the garden for years. More recently, people beyond the neighborhood had begun to notice, too, and a man from the newspaper had come by to talk to them and write a story about the garden. Janet's mother had her hair done in a new style and she bought a new dress for the interview.

"Since Janet's father is no longer with us," her mother told the reporter, "the garden has become a very special place to me and my daughter. It's a place where we can work together, where we can talk and make plans to make each year's growth better than the last."

I'd like to tell you what I think of the stupid garden, Janet thought. Instead, she just sat and looked glum and said nothing.

Janet's mother was especially fond of the geraniums with their kidney-shaped leaves and red, pink, or white flowers. Most of their geraniums would come back each spring, but there were always new places where she wanted to add new plants.

One early spring day, when Janet was thinking about summer camp and her mother was examining a cluster of salmon-colored blossoms on one of their geranium plants, her mother grew silent for a moment. She looked at Janet for a long time before speaking. "I wish you enjoyed working in the garden," she said, putting on her faint voice. "You're all I have now in the whole wide world. What am I going to do when you get older? What am I going to do when you go away to college and later, when you get married?"

"Maybe I can come by and help you tend the flowers once in a while," Janet said, not meaning it one bit. "That's still a long way off."

"Flowers can be like friends," her mother said. "I wish you appreciated them more."

And I wish you and your flowers were a thousand miles away, thought Janet.

Every day, when Janet came home from school, her mother insisted that they pull all the weeds and check the flowers to see that they weren't watered too little or too much. All Janet could think about was all the fun her friends were having.

One Saturday, when summer had nearly arrived, they worked especially hard to replant some of the budding plants in a part of the garden where they would look better. They worked for hours, stopping only to have lunch and, later, to have some lemonade. By dinnertime, Janet was very tired and more angry than she had ever been. Her knees and arms were sore, and the back of her neck was a little sun-burned—just enough to make her look strange if she wore a swimming suit.

"I'm going to bed early," she told her mother. "I don't feel well." I wish the garden and the house would burn down, she thought, walking up the stairs. I wish I could live anywhere else but here.

After she had a cool bath, Janet went to bed, and tried to think of ways she could run away forever. She thought of jumping on a truck, or hiding and pretending she'd been kidnapped. In spite of herself, however, she soon fell asleep. When she awoke, it was still dark. Turning to the lighted digital clock on her bed stand, she saw she had slept only a few hours, and it was still only a little after midnight.

She felt strange and uneasy, lying in the dark, staring at nothing but the clock and the pitch black beyond. She tossed one way and then another, but couldn't find a comfortable position. Her muscles were still sore, and the sunburn hurt. Finally, she decided to get a drink of water.

Passing the window in her room, Janet froze when she noticed a figure below in the flower garden, silhouetted in the silver spears of moonlight. The figure carried a candle, with the flame flickering in the light breeze. Her heart began to beat faster. She crouched below the windowsill and peeked again.

After several minutes, she recognized her mother, wearing the filmy, soft nightgown she always wore.

13

Her mother was walking slowly among the geraniums, and she appeared to be talking, although Janet could see no one else in the garden. Several times, her mother bowed and raised the candle high and said more things that Janet couldn't hear. Finally, Janet decided to go back to bed, and eventually she fell asleep.

"Why were you in the garden last night?" Janet asked the next morning, as they had breakfast together. "I got up during the night, and I'm sure I saw you."

"You must have been mistaken," her mother said. "I had a wonderful sleep all night. You must have dreamed it. Sometimes dreams can seem very real."

In school the following day, Janet was still thinking about it. The stupid garden is starting to give me bad dreams, she thought. When I grow up, I'm not going to have any flowers at all. Not one. Not even the plastic kind.

During lunch period, as she sat eating a peanut butter sandwich and thinking about her mother, the palm of her left hand itched. The more she scratched it, the more it itched. Finally, when it seemed that the itching would never stop, Janet examined her hand carefully. She gasped to see a tiny, green leaf growing out of her hand.

Closing her fist quickly, she went to her desk in home room, took a small pair of scissors and hurried to the girls' bathroom. She waited until no one was

14

in the room, then snipped off the leaf and tiny stem. It did not hurt to cut the stem, and when she did, the itching stopped. When she reached down to retrieve the leaf, she couldn't find it. For the rest of the day, she couldn't think of anything but the leaf. She was so frightened, she spoke to no one until she got home.

"I don't feel well," she told her mother. "I'm going to go to the bathroom, and then lie down."

In the upstairs bathroom, Janet nearly fainted when she looked into the mirror. Staring at herself, she saw tiny stems and the tiny, familiar round- and kidney-shaped leaves of geranium plants sprouting everywhere from her arms, legs, and neck.

Fighting the urge to scream and run in panic to the kitchen where her mother was cooking dinner, Janet instead grabbed the scissors from the drawer in the bathroom and began clipping the stems from her skin.

"Come down and eat, Janet," her mother called, when Janet was about halfway finished. "I hate to eat alone."

"I'll be there in a minute," Janet called, trying to sound as natural as possible. She could not tell her mother about the strange plants growing out of her skin. If she did, her mother might think she was totally crazy. Besides, her mother probably would take her to the doctor, and he might even put her in a mental hospital or something.

Moving as fast as she could, she clipped all the stems, then wrapped them in toilet paper and carried them to the trash can in the garage. Before going into the house to eat, she peeked again into the trash can, and the stems were gone. Maybe, she thought with a wild, sudden sense of fear, my mother and her garden finally are driving me mad.

During dinner, Janet kept sneaking glances at her hands and arms, but nothing appeared. Maybe it was just some kind of weird reaction or something, she thought. Maybe I'm allergic to something and don't know it.

"I'd really like to get to the mall tomorrow and look for jeans," she said, desperate to get away and think about something else for a change. "I talked to Sue Bernson, and she said her mother could take us out there right after school if you could bring us back later."

"I have some potting plants in the garage that really must be transplanted to the garden tomorrow," Janet's mother said. "Tomorrow's not a good time. I'll be tired, and besides, I could use your help. You should know that it takes a lot of work to have a truly fine garden."

"Mother . . ."

"I mean it. Not tomorrow. Sue Bernson and her mother can do what they want, but you're not going."

"I'm a prisoner in this house!" Janet screamed, throwing down her dinner napkin and rising from the table. "I'm sick to death of that garden. It's all we do! From spring until fall, the garden is the only thing that matters to you! I hate that garden!"

"Sit down!" commanded her mother. "You don't use that tone with me!"

"I won't!" screamed Janet, tears of anger streaming down her cheeks. "I hate that garden and I hate this house. I can't do anything but plant and pick and water and dig. I hate it! I hate everything you do! And I hate you!" She spun around, ran up the stairs and slammed the door of her room so hard two pictures fell to the floor. For several minutes she lay sobbing on the bed.

"You open this door this instant!" her mother finally called from the hallway. "You don't act that way in *my* house." It was the first time Janet had ever heard her mother call it *her* house.

"I *won't!*" screamed Janet. "I can't *wait* to get out of here! I'm calling Uncle Jim tomorrow and I'm going to ask him if I can live with him and Aunt Sandy. I don't *ever* want to work in that stupid garden again!"

Her mother said no more, and eventually Janet heard the door of her mother's bedroom close. She lay on her bed listening, but she heard no more sounds from her mother's room. For hours she lay there, still far too angry to go to sleep. Every few minutes she looked at the clock, until it finally showed a few minutes after midnight.

Still angry, but this time moving slowly and ever

so quietly, Janet tiptoed down the stairs and stepped silently into the garage, where she took the biggest, sharpest clippers she could find. Moving outside toward the garden, she felt the grass cold and wet under her bare feet.

At the edge of the garden, she paused for a moment. I've wanted to do this for a long, long time, she thought with a little thrill. I *hate* her, and I hate this garden . . .

Moving to the first flower, she whisked it off with a quick, clean swipe of the clippers. Moving along the row, she continued to clip until all the flowers lay in piles on the ground. Now she moved to other rows, clipping furiously, scattering more flowers like fallen soldiers about the ground as she worked. The more she clipped, the better she felt. Soon she was not even bothering to be very quiet, but instead clipping with wild abandon, slicing a blossom here, lopping off a bud there, until the entire garden was a large, barren patch filled with piles of green stalks and flowers.

Collapsing near an oak tree away from the garden, Janet threw the clippers aside. She had all she could do to keep from laughing out loud. She was panting from the exertion and her nightgown was all damp from perspiration and the dew. Although the ground was far lumpier than her bed, she soon fell asleep.

Some time later, Janet awakened with a start to the sound of her mother's voice. Rising up on one elbow, she realized that she was still in the grass under the tree, and night shadows still lay over the yard and the house.

Squinting in the moonlight, Janet saw her mother, holding a candle as before, standing in the garden. Just as before, her mother raised and lowered her head, again saying something Janet couldn't understand. To her astonishment, she suddenly realized that the flowers were standing in their perfect rows, uncut, as though Janet had never clipped a single blossom.

Soon her mother moved off again, as before, toward the house, her filmy nightgown fluttering softly in the gentle breeze.

Idly scratching her hand, Janet gasped again, and had everything she could do to keep from screaming loud enough for all the neighbors to hear. From her hands, arms, and legs, slim, green stems were growing. At the ends were leaves, some as large as three and four inches across, each with the familiar coarsely scalloped edges and soft, fuzzy surfaces she had seen so often on the geraniums in the garden.

Searching wildly for the clippers, Janet crawled through the grass as more stems, and more leaves, began to appear on her back and her neck and the top of her head. Opening her mouth to scream, she heard only a tiny, muffled sound as more tiny stems and leaves began to fill her mouth and throat, making it harder and harder to breathe. Rising to her feet, she stumbled sideways, then lurched forward as more

19

and more stems continued to grow from her, weighing her down. Finally she fell again. Through the leaves that now nearly covered her eyes she saw close-by the flowers of her mother's garden, waving gently as they had always waved.

A month or so later, Janet's mother sat in her kitchen, sipping coffee while a reporter from the newspaper talked to her again about her garden. While they talked, a photographer took pictures of the rows of flowers, moving happily in the sunlight.

"The disappearance of my only daughter has been a genuine tragedy," her mother said to the reporter. "As a mother, I still haven't gotten over it, of course, and never will. Like any mother, I never stop believing that she'll turn up. I'm glad I have the garden, though, which brings me comfort. I hope you understand: a garden can be a very comforting place at times like this."

Out in the garden, the photographer moved around and through the rows of marigolds, roses, daisies, tulips . . . and geraniums . . . snapping pictures, taking light measurements, humming as he worked.

Nearby, although he didn't notice, one of the geraniums was quite different from the others. If he'd looked closely, closer than anyone ever looked, he might have seen something very unusual. On the stalk, so tiny that it would have taken a very strong magnifying glass to see, were subtle hand- and leg-shaped lines. Within the flower was the tiniest outline of a face, twisted and frozen in a terrible, permanent image of fear.

If the photographer had known that this was a very special plant, and if he had leaned very, very close—which he, of course, didn't—he would have heard a tiny, tiny scream: "Help, Mom! Please! Help! I'm sorry! Please, Mom!"

THE VISIT OF JOSHUA SOMETHING

David was awake earlier than usual. It was, after all, the first day of school, and he didn't want to oversleep. He was excited, and a little nervous, too, about starting fourth grade. Michael, who was going into sixth grade, was still sound asleep. David jumped from his bed in the big upstairs room that the two brothers shared. He ran to his sleeping older brother and shook his shoulder.

"Michael," he said softly, then louder. "Michael! Get up! We have to eat breakfast. I don't want to be late! Don't you know what day it is?"

"Ummhhff," Michael mumbled. "Get out of here and leave me alone." He turned over and pressed his face deeper into the pillow.

"Michael's such a jerk," David said to his mother

as he slid his chair up to the kitchen table and reached for the toast. "He doesn't even know what day this is."

"Don't call names," she said gently. She pointed at the stairs. Michael was slowing moving down the steps, still looking half asleep.

"What's so exciting about school?" Michael said slowly, yawning as he pulled his chair up beside David's. "And then stupid David had to wake me up."

"Enough of that," their mother said. "No more fighting."

"All I wanted to tell him is there's a lot of new kids, and a lot of things to do," said David. "There's a new kid named Joshua in fourth grade. I know a kid who already met him. He's lived in different countries, and he's been all over. He knows different languages and stuff. He's even been to places like India and Egypt."

"What's his last name?" asked Michael.

"I don't know. Joshua something."

"Don't even know his name," said Michael.

"Oh, shut up, Michael!" said David.

"Enough!" said their mother, in a tone that showed she meant it.

Michael was feeling better and more lively when the bus finally arrived to take them to school. "Bye, Mom," he said. "Can you make us a surprise for a snack after school?"

Later that afternoon, David and Michael's mother was just putting a batch of fresh blueberry muffins into the oven when the boys burst through the front door.

"Hey, Mom!" said David. "Did you know there was an ancient Egyptian king who had a curse on the tomb where he's buried, and when some dudes opened it thousands of years later, they died?"

"Who told you that?" She turned from the oven.

"Joshua, the new kid," said David. "He knows a lot about history and stuff. Mr. Byrne, our teacher, said we'll be starting a unit on history tomorrow, and he was just like talking a little bit about it today and asking a few questions and stuff. You can't believe all the things Joshua knew. I told him maybe he could sleep over this weekend."

"Maybe," said their mother.

"You used to teach history, Mom," David said, deep in thought. "Did you ever hear about the curse on that guy's tomb?"

"Yes," she said, pulling a chair up to the counter. "His name was pronounced 'Toot-an-COM-en,' and it was spelled like this." She took a slip of paper and wrote T-U-T-A-N-K-H-A-M-E-N on it. "He lived around 3,350 years ago. He's called the 'boy king.' He was only nine years old when he became a king."

"Gosh, that's like me," said David.

"What a dumb king *you'd* make," said Michael, peeking through the oven door at the muffins. "You wouldn't even know how to give orders."

"Shut up, Michael," said David. "What about the curse, Mom?"

"Oh, that's an old story," she said, smiling. "There used to be a legend that whoever found and disturbed Tutankhamen's tomb, in a mysterious desert place in Egypt called the Valley of the Kings, would be cursed forever."

"Oh, oooooo, oh, ooooo," said Michael, fluttering his hands past David's face. "You shall diiieeee!"

David whacked Michael on the arm. "Shut up, Michael!" he said. "Just lemme alone. Did anybody ever find the tomb?"

"Yes." Their mother went back to the oven with a hot pad and began taking out the muffin tray. "Some people found it in this century, in 1922."

"Did they die?"

"Yes, supposedly the expedition leader and a couple of people in his group *did* die soon after, but it doesn't mean there was a curse. Lots of people who helped them didn't die. You can tell Joshua that."

The next Friday, after school, Joshua was waiting on the curb in front of his house when David, Michael, and their mother drove up.

"Looks like kind of a skinny little squirt," said Michael before they stopped the car. "Probably doesn't know how to do anything."

"*Sshh!*" hissed David. "You better be nice to him or I'm telling Dad."

"My mom said to tell you thanks for having me over," Joshua said, squirming in beside his new friends.

Michael watched Joshua as he spoke. Joshua seemed small and frail, even for fourth grade, although he certainly seemed bright enough.

"You ever play baseball?" Michael asked.

Before Joshua could answer, David said, "Joshua knows some other languages besides English. Right, Josh?"

"Naw, only a few words in Spanish and French," Joshua said, looking embarrassed.

"Know any French swear words?" Michael asked, smiling.

"Michael, enough!" said his mother.

"Want to maybe shoot some baskets later?" asked Michael, who was anxious to show this new boy how good he was at basketball.

"Sure," Joshua said, "but I'm not very good."

"Why don't you let your guest suggest a game?" said the boys' mother as they pulled into the driveway of their home.

"I know a little about chess and backgammon," said Joshua. "My dad taught me."

"Maybe you can show us how to play after we shoot some baskets," David said.

"Maybe we can try a little baseball later," Michael said. "I got a terrific glove for my birthday. We could get some kids together and have a game."

Later that evening, when they were getting ready for bed, David was still thinking about their new friend. "I guess he's okay," he whispered to his mother when she reached down to give him a good-night kiss. "He's a little different, though. He talks polite all the time, and I don't think he knows a darn thing about baseball."

"He's your guest," his mother whispered, "so you should play what *he* likes."

"How come you put him in the guest room, instead of here with us?" asked David.

"If he were in your room, he'd have to be on the floor in a sleeping bag. The guest room has more space and there's a nice bed. Now you go to sleep."

It was completely dark in the room when David awoke with a strong need to go to the bathroom. He could hear Michael sleeping, and he could see the red glow of the digital clock on the nightstand beside Michael's bed. The clock said 3:40 A.M.

David slipped to the floor and began feeling his way along the bed and along the wall to the door—the same way he had felt his way along the wall the other time he had had to get up at night, after chugging a full bottle of orange soda before going to bed.

He was moving down the hallway toward the bathroom when he noticed a faint needle of light peeking out from under the guest bedroom door.

As he moved closer, a faint sound made him catch his breath and stop. The sound coming from the room was of a very old man's voice, rising and falling softly, almost chantlike:

"Son of Amenophis and Tiye, from the land of the gods, I strike your enemies . . ."

David felt the hair on the back of his neck begin to rise. He ran into the bathroom, trying not to make any noise at all, then raced back to his and Michael's bedroom, flicking on the room light as he entered.

Putting his hand over Michael's mouth, he shook his brother roughly. "Wake up, Michael!" he whispered close to Michael's ear. "Wake up! There's some guy in Joshua's room! Wake up!"

Michael pushed David's hand away and tried to pull the covers over his head, but David held tight to his brother's mouth. Finally, Michael's eyes opened and he pulled free.

"What the heck are you doing . . ." he said half-aloud, but David again pressed his hand over his brother's mouth, motioning for him to be quiet.

"Some guy's in Joshua's room," David whispered. His eyes were wide and his hands were trembling. "Come and listen!"

The brothers turned off the room light again and crept slowly along the wall toward the guest room.

"I don't see any light," whispered Michael. "If you made this up, I'm gonna pound you tomorrow."

"Honest," said David. "Honest, there was light, and an old guy's voice."

As they reached the guest room door, they found only silence. No light showed under the door. Michael turned the knob ever so slowly and looked inside.

Joshua was sleeping peacefully. A slight breeze gently moved the window curtains as he slept.

"Stupid!" whispered Michael, after he and David again reached their room. "You probably dreamed it all."

"I did not!" whispered David. "There *was* some old guy in the room!"

The next morning, David and Michael's mother made a big breakfast, with lots of fruit and fresh muffins and hot cereal.

"David had this screwball dream or something last night," Michael started to say, but David kicked him under the table.

"Hey!" David said to Joshua. "Want to get a game going?"

"Sure," said Joshua. "But I told you, I'm not very good."

"Doesn't matter," said Michael. "Neither is my dorky brother, but he plays. I'll help you out."

That night, after they had roasted marshmallows over the grill in the backyard, Joshua said, "I had a terrific time. I hate to go home tomorrow."

Long after everyone had gone to bed and the house was quiet, David couldn't go to sleep. Finally he whispered, "Michael? Are you awake?"

There was no answer, so David waited several minutes more and whispered again. "Michael!" Still there was no answer.

David tried to go to sleep, and turned every way

he could, but still he remained wide awake. He tried switching the covers around, but nothing worked. Finally, after what seemed like hours, he decided to tiptoe into the hallway again and listen at Joshua's door.

As he reached the hallway, a cold chill settled over him, and once again the hair on the back of his neck began to stand on end. The needle of light peeked from under the door, just as before, and again he heard the murmuring of an old man's voice.

This time, instead of going to get Michael, he moved closer and slowly turned the knob on Joshua's door. As the door opened, a beam of light flooded outward from somewhere high in the room. Joshua stood on the floor near the bed, in the middle of the light. He was holding his hands high over his head, toward the mysterious light source, and his head was tipped back. His eyes were closed. David was startled to see that Joshua's face was no longer the face of a young boy, but that of a man.

"Son of Amenophis and Tiye," said the voice, as before. "From the land of the gods, I strike your enemies." Joshua was still wearing the same pajamas that David had lent to him the night before.

Joshua suddenly stopped his chant, as though sensing that someone else was in the room. He turned to David and looked at him with deep, glowing eyes that seemed to reach far, far back in time. David was too paralyzed with fear to move or speak.

Joshua motioned for David to come into the room. Although David's legs felt like lead, he moved slowly forward. His heart was beating very fast and he could feel a cold sweat forming on his back and forehead. He tried to speak but couldn't make a sound.

The figure gestured to David to sit down on the floor, and then he sat down cross-legged in front of him. When he spoke, his voice was deep and resonant and seemed to come to David over a long distance.

"Don't be afraid," said Joshua. "You must understand something, and you must listen carefully: Our souls live many lives. We are reborn as many different people."

David's throat was still too constricted to speak.

"You have lived before—hundreds, perhaps thousands of lifetimes," said Joshua.

"Who . . . are you?" asked David, in a near-whisper.

"I am a spirit-runner from the court of the ancient Egyptian god-king, Tutankhamen. I am sent to fulfill his curse. I have traveled far, and have far to go. I hunt those who defiled the tomb of my king."

David was now drenched in sweat. He began to inch slowly back, toward the door.

"Have no fear," Joshua said. His voice seemed to soften a little. "I have not come for you. Some of those I sought have gone forever to the Land of the Dead. Others have eluded me. Their spirits have fled throughout the earth, and some have lived several lifetimes. They may be anywhere. I am sworn to find them. Until I do, my king cannot rest." He paused again. "You must say nothing of this to anyone."

He turned, reached for the beam of light and began the chant again—"Son of Amenophis and Tiye . . ."—as David rose and backed slowly from the room.

In the hallway, David could feel his heart jumping in his chest like a frightened animal. He pinched his arm. "It's not a dream," he said out loud, his voice wavering.

Still drenched in cold sweat, he rushed into his parents' bedroom and shook his mother's arm. "Mom!" he whispered hoarsely, unable to conceal his fear. "Mom!"

She turned and reached out to touch his arm. "What is it, David? It's very late." She squinted in the dim light.

"Mom, I'm really scared!" His voice still shook with fear. "Joshua isn't really a kid, Mom. He's some kind of spirit-hunter or something who's hunting down the guys who messed up that tomb we were talking about. You know, the one with the curse."

"David, really . . ." She reached out with both arms and hugged him. "Why, you're shaking all over! And you're absolutely drenched! Oh, David, listen to me . . ." She hugged him tighter. "That's just a story. If I thought you'd have nightmares, I'd never have told . . ."

"Mom! It's real! He says we all live lots and lots of lifetimes and those guys are different people now and he's going all over tracking them all down! It's no dream, Mom!"

"Honey, I want you to go back to bed and try to think about something else. In the morning I'll make a nice breakfast for you and Joshua and Michael. Maybe some of those buttermilk pancakes you like."

"Mom!"

"I mean it, David. You're awake now. It was a dream. You go back to bed, and put all this out of your head. We all have to get some sleep."

Still trembling, David raced back to Joshua's room. He stopped before entering and looked for the slivers of light, but none came from under the door, as before. No whispered chants broke the silence. He turned the knob and peeked inside. In the hard shadows cast by the moonlight, it was difficult to see into the room. Moving forward slowly, he made out the outline of the bed with its rumpled sheets and fluffed pillow. The bed was empty.

Running back to his and Michael's room, he saw light streaming from beneath the door. Throwing it open, he screamed, an anguished, strangled scream that tore from deep inside him. Inside the room, suspended in a beam of light, Joshua had a firm hold on Michael, whose face was frozen in a soundless mask of fear. Together, the two figures were rising slowly, up and through the ceiling.

"No!" screamed David. "Mom! Mom! Please, Joshua! Not Michael! Not my brother! MOM . . . !"

THE RADIO

Tom hated to admit it, but he was bored.

School was out, and that was great, but now it was hard sometimes to find something to do. He was still waiting for the coach to call about summer soccer practice. His older brother, Jeff, was gone all the time to the beach with his surfboard and his friends. Tom's mom only let him play Nintendo a half hour a day, and there wasn't always somebody around to do things with.

Teddy and Kevin, the twins from around the corner, came over when they could, and that was okay. They'd shoot baskets, or get out their guitars and drums and try to play like a rock band, or sometimes the three of them took their bikes down to 7-Eleven for a Coke. But now Teddy and Kevin said their parents were sending them to some stupid camp for a week. It looked like he was going to be alone again.

"Summer ain't so great," Tom said to Jeff one day, after a carload of Jeff's friends dropped him and his surfboard off at home. Tom was sitting on the front steps with his chin in his hands.

"That's cause you got a year or two to go before Dad will let you go to the beach by yourself," Jeff said. "Don't worry about it. I used to get bored once in a while, too. You just gotta find somethin' to do."

"Yeah. Like what?" Tom said, without lifting his chin.

"I dunno. You could get a job like lawn mowing and make a few bucks."

"Great. Real fun."

"Well, *I* dunno," said Jeff, sounding a little irritated. "You could try a hobby or something. Maybe build something. I used to build model airplane kits, and it used to be kinda fun, once you got into it."

"I don't like model airplanes."

"Well, I don't know, then," Jeff said, placing his surfboard in its rack in the garage. "Ask Dad. Sometimes he knows a few things to do."

"Dad," Tom said later, during dinner, "what did you do when you were a kid and you didn't have anything to do?"

"Well, lots of things," said Tom's dad, pushing his chair back and thinking for a moment. "I remember I built a radio once when I was around your age. It

35

had two tubes in it. They don't even have tubes now. I can't tell you how excited I was when I heard the first scratchy voices and some music come out of the little speaker. It was like I'd performed some kind of magic."

"Did it take you long?"

"Naw. Piece o' cake. Uncle Jerry helped me. If you ever want to do something like that, I could help. They have neat kits in the radio store. No tubes. Everything snaps into place. I saw 'em when we were looking at VCRs."

"I dunno." Tom looked at Jeff. "Wish I could surf. Jeff messes around at the beach all day and does what he wants."

"Yeah, well, in a year or two you'll be a studly dude like me and you can," Jeff said, grinning and kissing his own arm. "Try the radio. It's better'n sittin' around on your butt."

"Studly dude," Tom said. "What a nerd."

"I'll even pay for the kit," Tom's dad said. "I'd just like to see if you can do it."

"Probably can't," said Jeff, "considering you're a hopeless bonehead."

At the store, Tom still wasn't convinced. The clerk was a skinny guy who looked like he built his own supercomputers.

"Several types of radio kits are available," he said to Tom's dad, "including shortwave, VHF police-band

36

radios, and crystal kits. You can put them all together easily at home."

Tom was wishing they could leave. Yard work might even be better than this.

"On the other hand," the clerk continued, "if you want something more, we have complete lab kits like this one." He pointed at a red-and-blue, plastic-wrapped box. "You can build everything from a radio to a Morse Code outfit to a magnetic noise detector."

That sounded a little more interesting than the radios, Tom thought.

The clerk seemed anxious to tell all about the kit. "It has all the premounted transistors, capacitors, resistors, and diodes," he said. "Just spend a little time putting it all together and you have your own electronic laboratory."

"What do you think?" said Tom's dad. "Like it?"

Tom nodded. He certainly didn't feel as enthusiastic about the kits as his dad and the store clerk seemed to be.

"Great," said his dad, who sounded happier than Tom was.

Well, maybe this *is* a little more interesting than I thought, Tom said to himself that evening as he snapped components into coded, spring-mounted slots in the plastic base. He was starting to get a little excited about hearing the radio play for the first time.

The next morning, he even got up earlier than usual to work on the kit, and by dinnertime he was finished. Placing the tiny earphone in his ear, he flicked the radio switch. At first he heard a faint crackle and then a voice, small and nasal, squeaked out of the earphone. Dad was right, he thought. This really *is* kinda fun, hearing it work for the first time.

"Tom, come and eat," his mother called from downstairs.

"Just a minute," he yelled. "I want to try something." He fiddled with the wires, to make certain they were connected, then fiddled with the controls. The tiny voice grew larger in the earphone.

"In today's news," it said, "arsonists are blamed for a fire that destroyed Hannay's Market near Fifth and Drake streets on the city's near-east side. The fire, which may have been set late Sunday night or early Monday morning, was discovered by employees when they reported for work . . ."

The next day, at dinner, Tom's dad said to his mother, "Honey, remember Hannay's Market where we used to shop when we were first married? Down on Drake Street? It burned this morning. Total loss."

"Oh, yeah," Tom said. "People found it burning when they went to work. I heard them tell about it yesterday on the radio kit."

"No, son," said his dad. "It happened this morning. I just heard it coming home, on the car radio."

Instead of arguing, Tom just shrugged and began

picking at the chicken drumstick on his plate. After dinner, he went back to his room and took out the kit again. Maybe I can find some rock stations, he thought. No matter how hard he tried, he found only news. And always it was the same announcer. Either this radio gets only one station, thought Tom, or that guy gets around a lot.

"A lone gunman held up the downtown offices of Superior Federal Savings this afternoon," said the announcer's voice. "Brandishing a pistol, he escaped with an undetermined amount of cash." Dropping the kit on his bed, Tom raced downstairs.

"What's the name of the savings and loan where you work?" he asked his dad, who was reading the paper in the family room.

"Superior Fed," said his dad. "Why?"

"My gosh!" said Tom. "Why didn't you tell us about the robbery?"

"What robbery?" said his dad.

"They just said Superior Federal was robbed today," said Tom, disappointed. "You mean nothing happened in your office?"

"Just a normal day. They probably said some other savings place that sounded like 'Superior.' "

A day later, Tom was in the garage tightening the chain on his bike when his dad got home. Before he got out of the car, Tom noticed that he was pale and nervous-looking.

"Robbery today, Honey," he said, walking into the

kitchen where Tom's mother was preparing dinner. "I didn't call you from work. I figured it would just upset you."

Tom's mother put down a bowl she was holding and hugged his dad. "I'm so glad you're safe," she said.

"Dad, I told you about the robbery *yesterday*," Tom said, suddenly aware of a strange feeling growing in the pit of his stomach.

"Son, that was a simple mistake." His dad plopped into a chair and pulled off his tie. "You just heard wrong, or maybe you were picking up a signal from someplace else."

"What was it like?" Tom asked.

"Just one robber," said his dad. "In and out of the place in less than three or four minutes. Had a gun. Pretty darn scary. You never know if those idiots are on drugs or something."

Tom could hardly wait to get up to his room and try the radio again. During dinner he ate almost nothing, despite the fact that his mother had made lasagna, his all-time favorite. All he could think about was the radio.

"Dad," he asked, when they were almost finished with dinner, "do you think it's possible to tell the future—to tell things that are going to happen, before they do?"

"Oh, I guess some people think they can, but I've never seen anything that made me believe you can," said his dad. "A lot of these nut cases think they can read your eyeball or something and tell you what's gonna happen to you tomorrow, but I'm pretty doubtful. I think it's smarter to stick to facts about today, not guesswork about tomorrow."

Tom decided he wouldn't tell them about the radio.

Back in his room, he placed the tiny plug in his ear. Again he heard the familiar voice. "A seven-car pileup on the Beltline Freeway during rush hour this morning caused many motorists to be delayed for as much as two hours in getting to work downtown . . ."

Tom pulled the plug from his ear and went back downstairs. "Don't take the Beltline Freeway to work tomorrow morning, Dad," he said. "There's going to be a big seven-car pileup that could make you as much as two hours late."

"How do you know this?" asked his dad, sounding a little doubtful.

"Well . . ." He wasn't sure he should tell. "Well, it's the radio in my kit, Dad. It . . ."

His dad smiled. "What did you build with the kit? A crystal ball to tell the future?"

"Dad, it's just that the radio . . ."

"Look, son. There's nobody who can predict things like seven-car accidents. Just have fun with your kit and enjoy it, but don't get weird and try to tell the future."

When he came home from work the next day, Tom's dad came straight to Tom's room. "How did

41

you know about the freeway accident?" he asked. "I was an hour and a half late to work. When I got there, I remembered what you said yesterday. How did you do it?"

"Just did, I guess," Tom said. I won't tell anyone about the radio after all, he thought to himself. It's more fun to let people think I have special powers . . .

Over the next several weeks, Tom astounded his dad and other people by accurately predicting accidents, big-league baseball scores, news headlines, weather, and other events. Gradually, word of Tom's "special powers" began to reach beyond their house and neighborhood.

Soon newspaper people were coming every night to talk and take photographs of Tom. Pictures of him were published in magazines, and piles of letters began to arrive from all over the country. Even some famous people wrote to him with words of advice and encouragement. Still, he told no one about the radio.

Many of the letters that came to Tom asked for help. Some people were going to have operations, and they wanted to know if they would come through all right. Others wanted to take plane trips, and wanted to be certain that no accidents were going to occur.

"I can't help all these people," Tom finally said in frustration. "I just wish they'd stop bothering me."

For a while, he quit listening to the radio, and quit making predictions. Gradually, the number of calls and letters dropped off. "If people want help, they can go to someone else," Tom said. "Sometimes I wish none of this had ever happened."

For a while, he thought about secretly destroying the radio, just smashing it and throwing it out in the trash. Then one day he had an idea. Why not, he thought to himself, bet lots and lots of money on horse races, football games, and other sporting events? Since I'd already know who won, I could get tons of money . . .

"That's fine, except it's cheating," Jeff said when Tom revealed the idea to him. "If you have the power to know the future, then you'd have an unfair advantage over other people who were betting."

"So what?" Tom said. "What are they going to do?"

"It just seems like you oughta be helping people instead of trying to cheat them," Jeff said.

"It's none of your business," Tom snapped. "I heard about some men who will take my information and place bets, and give me money when they win. I could buy a jet ski and season baseball tickets and all kinds of stuff if I had a lotta money."

"Have you talked to Dad about this?" asked Jeff. "He wouldn't allow it."

"No," said Tom, "and I'm not going to. And if you mention anything to him, these men probably will come out here and beat you up."

"Well, I'm going surfing," said Jeff. "Try to get your head on straight. I still think caring about people is more important than stupid money."

That's what you think, thought Tom. He went to his room and decided he would start right away to listen to all the sporting news.

A short while after he placed the plug in his ear, he heard the announcer say, ". . . and in horse racing, a tremendous upset at Santa Anita today, with a horse named Fair Oaks winning, paying twenty dollars back for every dollar bet. No one expected Fair Oaks to come even close to winning . . ."

Wow! thought Tom. That means if somebody bet a thousand dollars on Fair Oaks, he'd get *twenty thousand dollars* back! I gotta tell Jeff, and see if he knows anybody who has some money! We can bet it all! I gotta catch Jeff and convince him before he leaves!

He threw the radio toward the bed and sprinted down the stairs. "Jeff!" he yelled. "Jeff! Wait up!" As he ran through the kitchen, he spotted Jeff and his friends turning out of the driveway and heading down the street with their surfboards strapped to the top of the car. "Jeff!" he yelled again, bursting out the back door and leaping across the yard after the moving car. "Wait up!"

Upstairs, in Tom's room, the radio leaned against one leg of the bed where it fell. The switch was still on. From the earphone on the floor came a tiny, tiny voice.

"In local news," it said, "a youth who recently had gained fame with his ability to forecast the future was killed near his home yesterday when he apparently ran into the street into the path of an oncoming truck . . ."

THE DAM

Most of the students in Miss Woods' fifth-grade class had arrived at Terrance Elementary School before dawn. They stood with their parents in small groups, stamping their feet against the chill air. Some waited in cars, out of the wind. The sun was just beginning to wink on the far eastern horizon.

"I hate to get up so early," Becky said, jumping up and down on the sidewalk near her friend, Chris. "When I get up this early, I feel tired all day."

"I just wish we didn't have such a long bus ride," said Chris, pulling her sweater up and folding her arms more tightly in front of her. "I just really hate long, boring bus rides."

"Miss Woods said yesterday we can stop and get

a burger on the way back," said Becky. "That way we won't like totally starve."

"Robert Driesel's mother probably gave him about ten dollars again," said Chris. "She always gives him so much money, and he's always buying more malts and junk than he can eat."

"Robert's such a nerd," said Becky.

"There's Miss Woods now," Chris said as their teacher's station wagon came into view.

More parents began getting out of cars and talking with each other while the class got in line to board the bus. Becky and Chris hurried in and grabbed good seats by the window halfway back. They were talking, and didn't realize until too late that they were seated directly in front of Ryan Anderson.

"Oh, yecch!" whispered Chris. "Look who's behind us! Remember last year, he put his plastic fake vomit on the bus seat, and he tried to slip that gopher snake into your lunch bag!"

The girls were about to ask to move when Miss Woods stood up and began to speak in the front of the bus.

"We'll be on the road about two hours this morning and about two hours this afternoon coming back," she said. "I know it's a long trip, but it should be fun. Today, we're going to go up across the Idaho border to see the new Tahachi Dam on the Snake River. How many of you have seen a large river dam before?"

A few people raised their hands.

"I saw the Hoover Dam two years ago," said one boy.

"Good," said Miss Woods. "The Tahachi Dam is a concrete arch-gravity dam, very much like the Hoover Dam on the Colorado River, except that the Tahachi Dam is not quite so large. It's still big, though, and furnishes hydroelectric power to lots of people in this part of the country. It rises several hundred feet on one side from the river, and is made of thousands of tons of concrete."

Becky and Chris already were looking out the window at the cars passing by. Neither was very interested in dams and rivers.

"I can't wait until we stop for burgers," said Chris. "My mom gave me three dollars."

"Some of you may not be very interested in dams," Miss Woods continued, "but you may find something very interesting about this dam. It isn't very old, but already there is a legend about it."

"What kind of legend?" said Lisa, who was sitting in the front seat, near the driver, Mr. Carling.

"Well," said Miss Woods, "it took several hundred men a long time to build the dam. While they were working on the project, a terrible accident happened. It was necessary to pour thousands of tons of concrete to form the dam. One afternoon, one of the workers, a young man who was helping to pour the foundation, tripped on an iron bar that was sticking out and fell

48

into the soft concrete. Before he could be pulled out, he was covered with tons and tons of concrete."

"What did they do?" asked Ryan.

"There was nothing they could do to save him," said Miss Woods, "so they left his body there, sealed forever inside the dam."

"Neat!" said one boy.

"That's awful," said several girls.

Miss Woods' voice took on a mysterious tone. "People around the dam have reported some strange things just in the few years since the dam was completed."

"What sort of strange things?" said Becky.

"Well," Miss Woods smiled, "many people have said that on certain nights, a shadowy figure of the same young man can be seen walking slowly across the top of the dam."

"I don't know if I believe that," said Ryan.

"Several people have reported the same thing," said Miss Woods. "It's even been in the newspapers."

"That gives me the creeps," said Lisa. "What does he do?"

"He just walks slowly back and forth," said Miss Woods. "Everyone who's seen him says he's still wearing work clothes and a construction hat, just like he had on when the accident happened, except you can see right through him. When anybody comes close, he just vanishes."

"I don't think I want to visit this dam," said Becky.

"Me either," said Lisa.

"No need to worry," said Miss Woods, still smiling. "Nobody ever has proven that the story is true, and besides, he's only been seen at night. We'll be there in broad daylight." Then she added, "I've told you enough about the Tahachi Dam for now. I'll give you some facts and figures when we get there, about the dam and why it was built. For now, though, I want you to stay in your seats and keep the noise level down until we get there."

"What do you think?" said Ryan, leaning forward toward Becky and Chris. "Think it's true? Maybe it's like his ghost or soul can't leave, or something."

"Yeah, weird," said Chris.

When the bus finally approached the graveled parking lot near the dam, Miss Woods stood up again. "I want you to listen carefully," she said. "We have to stick together as a group. We can't be fooling around and going off somewhere. This is extremely important. It's especially dangerous on the walkway along the top railing. There's a cement wall, but it isn't very high, so no leaning over and no fooling around. It's a sheer drop of more than 470 feet, straight down to the rocks and the river below."

"I hate heights," said Lisa.

"If you're scared, just don't go near the railing," said Lisa's friend, Kim.

"I don't mind heights at all," Becky said to Chris. "I used to wish I could be an aerialist in the circus and walk way up on the high wire and have all those people cheering."

"When we've seen the view from the top, we'll go over to the Visitors' Center," said Miss Woods. "They have some snacks and souvenirs, and bathrooms are there, too. Now, everyone follow me, and stay close."

Walking along the path to the top of the dam, they felt a cool, clover-scented breeze off the surrounding hills. Far below them, they could hear the sounds of the river spilling and bursting over the rocks. A few tourists strolled on the dam near the cement wall and railing. Some were snapping pictures of the view. Others were taking pictures of each other.

"I'm not so sure, Miss Woods," said Lisa as the group approached the walkway and started across. Her face was pale and she was trembling a little.

"It's all right. Just hold my hand," Miss Woods said. "We'll stay away from the railing."

"I don't think I can," Lisa said, looking first up and down the walkway, and then over at the rest of her class.

"Sure you can," said Miss Woods, taking her hand and starting to guide her forward. Most of the class members were already on the walkway, moving toward the center of the dam.

"No, I'm sorry!" Lisa cried. She wrenched her hand away from Miss Woods and began running back toward the parking lot and the bus.

"Lisa! Lisa, please!" Miss Woods called. "Stay right here, and don't go any farther until I get back," she yelled to the class as she ran after Lisa.

"I don't know what she's so scared about," said Becky as they watched Lisa run toward the bus with Miss Woods close behind. "There's a wall and a rail and all. No big deal."

"Well, it *is* a little scary when you look over," said Chris. "You could drop something and it would take a long time before it hit the water."

"Naaa," said Becky. "It's only scary if you *think* it's scary. Watch this." She looked up and down the walkway, then hopped up on the wall, with one foot planted on each side of the rail.

"Are you crazy?" hissed Chris. "Get down before you get in real trouble."

With several of the class watching her, Becky began to step along the top of the wall, smiling and raising her hands like an aerialist. "Just like the circus," she said, still smiling.

"Becky!" Miss Woods screamed from the distant parking lot where she finally had caught up with Lisa. "Get down this instant!"

"What did she say?" Becky turned around, toward the bus and Miss Woods. As she did so, her foot caught on the top edge of the railing and she lost her balance. Her arms waving wildly, she screamed and the class gasped in stunned silence as she teetered a moment, then plunged over the edge, still screaming as she fell toward the river and the rocks below.

"No! Oh, no, no, no, no, no!" Miss Woods screamed as she ran back toward the walkway.

Many of the shocked class members began to shriek in disbelief, and several of the nearby tourists ran over to the spot where Becky had been. The bus driver, Mr. Carling, bolted from the bus and ran to the Visitors' Center, yelling for someone to call the police. Two young men from the Center rushed to the walkway and leaned over, trying to see Becky below.

"Can you see her?" cried several children. "Where is she?"

Miss Woods moved among the children, weeping and moaning, tears streaking down her cheeks. She clasped and unclasped her hands, then began hurrying them all away from the walkway and back toward the bus. "Now you *stay* here," she yelled, her voice strained, "and *don't move!*" Then she ran back to the walkway and grasped one of the Visitors' Center employees by the arm. "Where? Where?" she yelled. "Do you see her?"

Within minutes a police car roared into the parking lot and two officers ran to the railing. "Have you spotted her?" one called out as they ran. Through the open patrol car windows, staccato voices and radio static raked over the sobbing children and covered the distant sound of the rushing river.

"Yeah, there she is," shouted one of the Visitors' Center employees. "There's the body, over by the edge. Looks like it's caught between a couple of rocks."

At the bus, the children milled about, sobbing, hugging each other, and pacing until dust rose around them like a low fog. Chris sat in the powdery dirt, crying uncontrollably. She leaned against one of the bus tires and buried her face in her hands. She had never felt so horrible in her life.

It was near dusk as the motor home pulled into the broad, paved parking lot near the top of the Tahachi Dam.

"What do you think, Christine?" said the driver. "Want to come with me and the kids and see what it looks like?"

"No," said the woman, gazing across the walkway to the hills beyond. "It's been twenty-five years, and I still feel kind of uneasy up here. I'll just wait for you. *You keep an eye on the children.*"

"I will, honey," said Christine's husband. "We'll just take a few minutes to look around. Now stay close by me, kids. We don't want any accidents."

"Come on, Mom," called Drew. He motioned to his brother, Matt, and their younger sister, Tina. "Let's go look at the dam."

"I've seen the dam," said Christine, "many years ago, and I don't want to see it again. Now you hurry. It's almost dark and we have to get going."

As she sat in the sudden silence, she remembered the shock and the screams and the horrible feeling of that day. "You were my best friend, Becky," she said softly to herself. "I wonder what you might have become, what you might have grown into."

After several minutes, she noticed that evening darkness was quickly settling in over the dam. She got out of the motor home and tried to spot her family on the walkway. "I don't know why I ever agreed to come here," she said aloud, to no one. "We have to get out of here, now, before night settles in. I hate this place."

"Jim!" she called out. Now she could see her husband and the three children strolling along the far end of the walkway. "Jim!" They were too far away to hear.

Fear began to set in as she approached the familiar wall and the railing. The voices came back to her, out of the long-distant past. Children's screams, the yells of the police officers, Miss Woods sobbing . . .

"Jim!" she called again, waving toward her family. "Let's get going."

Her husband and children saw her and waved back. They continued to stroll along, pointing at the river and the hills beyond.

She felt her throat constrict and a deepening feeling

of dread as she stood on the walkway. "I have to get away from here," she told herself. "I've got to get away . . ."

She turned toward the motor home, walking quickly, then stopped and turned back toward the walkway, waving again at her family as she did so. She could scarcely make out their figures in the growing darkness.

"Jim!" she called again, her voice straining. "Jim! We have to leave!"

She stopped and stood a moment near the walkway. With a shriek of laughter, Matt suddenly burst out of the darkness, then Drew, chasing him with a dead bird. Within seconds, Jim followed, smiling.

"Where's Tina?" said Chris, unable to conceal her rising fear.

"I thought she ran ahead with the boys," said Jim, reaching out to take hold of Chris' arm. "Don't worry. I'll go get her." He turned and disappeared again, while Drew and Matt ran off toward the motor home.

In the near-total dark, Chris suddenly gasped, reaching out to the wall to steady herself. A few yards from her, Tina appeared out of the darkness, walking slowly along the top of the wall, with one foot on each side of the rail. Slightly behind her, two filmy, silent figures moved with her along the top of the wall. One was tall, a young man, wearing a construction hat and work clothes. The other was a small girl, smiling and

56

stepping along beside him, holding her hands high in the manner of a tightrope walker.

"Jim!" she screamed, rushing to scoop Tina from the railing and hug her close to her. Her voice was ragged and strained in the cold air. "Jim!"

At the sound of her voice, the figures on the wall stopped and stared at her. The girl lowered her arms, then smiled as she raised a hand to wave slowly in Christine's direction.

"What's the matter, Mom?" asked Tina as Jim ran up to them and put his arms around them both. "What's wrong? Why are you crying, Mom?"

It was a moment before she could speak. "I'll tell you sometime. Right now, I just want to go away from here. Please, Jim!"

Driving away, Christine turned and looked one last time as the walkway faded from sight in the night air. As she did, she saw them again, strolling on the wall. Before Christine closed her eyes, the figure of Becky turned once more, still smiling, and waved good-bye before vanishing into the darkness.

THE MUSIC TEACHER

Many years ago, in the beautiful Black Forest of what is now Germany, in a small city (the name of which really isn't very important), lived a small, mostly ordinary girl named Elsa. She had long, brown hair and a pleasant smile, and she did mostly ordinary things. She studied in school, got mad at boys, had girl friends with whom she laughed and shared secrets, and she dreamed many dreams.

Elsa's favorite dream was that she would one day play the piano before great and important audiences. Except for music, she received mostly average, ho-hum grades. In music, however, she was very skilled.

What also wasn't very ordinary about Elsa was that she had no parents. Neither her father nor her mother was known, since Elsa had been found as a baby at the doorstep of the city's only orphanage. "Please take care of my baby daughter," said a note from her mother pinned to Elsa's blanket. "I have no money for food, and if you don't take her, she will die."

As an orphan, Elsa lived with many other children who also had no parents. They all lived in the same large brick building. The girls all slept in one big room, with their beds in long, severely neat rows, and the boys all slept in another large room in a distant part of the building. Everyone, girls and boys alike, ate their meals by candlelight on heavy wooden tables in a large dining room in which talking was not allowed before, during, or after meals. Those who violated rules were publicly spanked with a large leather strap.

The only times Elsa and the other orphans were allowed out of the orphanage were to go to church— a large, cold, dusty church on top of a steep hill—and to go to school—which also was a cold and dusty building attached to the church. The grown-ups in the church and the school were mostly distant, humorless people with pinched-in faces and a look as though they had been eating sour fruit all their lives.

Elsa and a few of the other children were allowed out of the orphanage for one other purpose: Once a week, a small group of children who, like Elsa, were outstanding music students were permitted to walk to the home of a famous music teacher to study piano.

The teacher, a small, angry-faced woman named Frau Gruber, had a slightly humped back and lived in a tiny cottage outside the city with an enormous giant Schnauzer dog named Otto (whose temper was generally as foul as his owner's). The cottage, surrounded by dense thorn bushes, seemed to contain space only for Frau Gruber's bedroom, a small kitchen, and the music room. In this room was her most prized possession: an immense, hand-carved Glueckmann piano with lion's-foot legs and highly polished ivory and ebony keys.

Students privileged to study with Frau Gruber were expected to be strictly on time and to have their lessons perfectly prepared. While each was playing, the others were expected to sit in complete silence. None was permitted to speak unless spoken to by Frau Gruber. This was fine with most of the students, since they were too frightened to speak, anyway. Although they were afraid, they knew that Frau Gruber was the finest teacher in the city, perhaps in all of Europe.

"This is *pianissimo*," she would say, almost whispering the musical term as her fingers softly caressed the keys like a tailor examining silk. "And *this* is *fortissimo!*" she would shout, striking the keys and making the students jump.

Although the students were not permitted to speak during lessons, they always talked among themselves while walking to and from the little cottage.

"She's the devil's bride, a witch," Klaus said each time they left to go back to the orphanage. Klaus was the only boy in Elsa's tiny group of students, and the only boy she considered a friend at the orphanage. Klaus was strong and athletic, and he had been punished many times, both by Frau Gruber and by the school, for breaking rules. He also was a promising musician, which is why Frau Gruber permitted him to continue studying with her.

"She makes me cry sometimes," Teresa, Elsa's best friend, said one day. "I love music more than anything else in the world, but I hate studying with her." Teresa was frail and fine-featured and rarely raised her voice, even when angry. She also had frequent colds and many allergies.

"Don't let her bother you," Elsa said, patting Teresa on the arm. "Long after you've forgotten Frau Gruber, you'll still have your music."

"To be called 'Frau,' she must have been married," Teresa said. "How could anyone ever have married someone so cranky?"

"I heard she was married, but her husband left her," said Katrina, who was one of the other students.

"Haven't you heard?" said Klaus, eager to share a fresh nugget of information. "I thought everyone had heard the story that the old people of the city whisper about Frau Gruber."

"Not another witch story," Elsa said, smiling and pushing at Klaus' arm.

"Really," said Klaus, pausing and looking over his shoulder. "I heard this from Frau Hanfstangl, the orphanage cook, who made me promise never to tell anyone. They say that long ago, when Frau Gruber was young, she had a lover. She also had an ambition—to be the best pianist in the land. After she and her lover were married, she was still ambitious, so she consulted an evil sorcerer. The sorcerer showed her how to sell her husband's soul—not her own—to the devil. The devil repaid her by helping her to become a great pianist and music teacher."

"And what of her husband?" asked Katrina.

"The thought that the devil now owned his soul drove him mad," Klaus said. "It is said he still wanders the countryside, sleeping in haystacks, eating scraps, vowing vengeance upon the woman who sold his soul."

"I still say there are no sorcerers and no spells," Elsa laughed. "Frau Gruber is simply an old and cranky teacher."

As the weeks passed, Elsa looked forward each time to meeting Klaus, Teresa, and the others in front of the orphanage steps to begin the walk to Frau Gruber's cottage. Sometimes they didn't talk about music at all. Sometimes they talked about how Frau Hanfstangl had more than once almost dipped her large bust in the soup kettle while reaching for things on her stove. Other times they talked about who might some day adopt them. Everyone dreamed of being selected by a kind and wealthy merchant or nobleman and going off to live on a fine country estate.

More often than not, however, the conversation came back to Frau Gruber. "She's a dark witch, a sorceress," Klaus always said. "If she wanted to, she could turn tin into gold, or dogs into hawks. And besides, she has terrible breath."

This always made Elsa laugh. "All we know for certain," she said, "is that Frau Gruber knows how to turn students into pianists."

One day during the lesson Frau Gruber announced that she might have to retire soon and quit teaching because she was getting too old and tired for the work.

"I *hate* having to retire, and I *HATE* growing older!" Frau Gruber cried out suddenly, banging her fist on the beautiful piano keys and startling everyone. For the rest of the lesson she was moody and distracted, and seemed to pay little attention as the students played.

The next lesson day when Elsa and the others met at the orphanage steps, Teresa was missing.

"Probably another cold," Katrina said.

"Probably Frau Gruber has her boiling in a pot," said Klaus, but no one laughed.

During the following lesson, Frau Gruber was the picture of cheerfulness, bouncing and fluffing about the music room and showing the children in grand style exactly how each piece should be played. She even smiled a few times.

"Because you've done so well today," she said, smiling again her slow, pinched smile, "I'll reward you by playing a composition I've written. I've decided to name it after your little friend—what was her name? Oh, yes. Teresa."

Elsa gasped in surprise, but sat quietly as Frau Gruber played the new piece. It was a beautiful, soft lullaby, the tones of which rose and fell like gentle spring rain.

"That was beautiful," Elsa said when it was finished, forgetting for a moment the rule about not speaking unless spoken to.

Frau Gruber nodded, then walked from the room and did not punish Elsa. As she turned to leave, Elsa paused by the piano. Reaching out to touch the music, Elsa was overcome with a strange and uncomfortable sense of dread.

"Do not touch the music," commanded Frau Gruber, walking back into the room. "No one is to touch my music."

Walking back to the orphanage, Elsa could not rid herself of the terrible feeling she had felt when reaching out to touch the new music.

For the next several days, no one could find Teresa, in spite of the fact that people from the orphanage and school searched every corner and closet where she might have been. People from the orphanage even retraced the route to Frau Gruber's cottage, and talked to Frau Gruber about Teresa's disappearance. Still, Teresa remained missing. Those who ran the orphanage said that she must have run away, perhaps with passing Gypsies.

At the next lesson, Elsa was even more startled when Klaus failed to appear. Again, Frau Gruber was the picture of cheerfulness, this time playing a new piece she called "Klaus." It was a rousing march, full of strong, thumping rhythms and cascading flourishes.

"Now, I'm worried," Elsa said to the others during the walk back to the orphanage. When Klaus remained missing after several days, she became even more worried. "I'm almost afraid to go back to Frau Gruber's," she told Katrina, "for fear I'll end up missing, too."

"Maybe there's some truth to what Klaus said about the sorcerer," said Katrina, her eyes wide with fear. "But the only one who knows for certain is Frau Gruber's husband."

The next day, when her work was done, Elsa decided to sneak out of the orphanage and try to find the madman who had once been Frau Gruber's husband. I *have* to try something, she told herself, before I go back to that cottage . . .

Walking quickly, she was soon out of the city, and began to look around every haystack, bridge, and thicket she could find until night fell. She knew people from the orphanage would be looking for her. She would have to search quickly when the sun came up the next morning before she was caught. She found a patch of soft river reeds near a tiny stone bridge and made herself comfortable. Soon she was asleep.

After what seemed no time at all, she opened her eyes to see the sun inching up over the far eastern horizon. She was still quite comfortable in her bed of reeds beside the little river. While she was thinking about what she should do, she heard a distant coughing and a commotion on the other side of the bridge, at the far edge of the river. Squinting in the early light, she saw a dirty, stooped-over figure of a man with a long, gray and very dirty beard, poking at pieces of food thrown away by passersby.

"It's disgusting, that's what it is!" the man said, poking at the food. "And it's wasteful, too." He coughed more, then sat down and began to eat some of the scraps.

Elsa at first was afraid to say anything, but remembering that she might be found soon by people from the orphanage, she stood up and called to the man across the river.

"Excuse me, Sir," she called. "I'm looking for the husband of Frau Gruber."

"Of course you are," said the man without looking up from the scraps of food. "Don't you think I know that?"

"I don't know how you know that, since I just now told you," said Elsa, thinking that the man was very rude.

"I know more than you think," said the man, still looking at his food. "And I know why you're here. Now you come over to this side, because I'm an old man and you're not, and I'm tired."

Elsa was a little frightened to approach him, but she did so in spite of her fears. She stopped several arms' lengths away. Even at that distance, she could tell by the smell that he had not bathed for a very long time. His eyes were fiery red and his eyebrows were thick and bushy-white. He picked at the scraps of castaway food with dirty fingers, pausing occasionally to smack his lips when he found a particularly tasty-looking morsel.

"Well, who do you think I am? The Christmas Elf?" he snapped at her, still without looking up.

"I don't know," Elsa said, "but if you know where I can find Frau Gruber's husband, I would be obliged if you'd tell me."

"Of course I know where he is!" barked the old man. "Don't you think I know where he is?"

Elsa, who now was near tears, began to back away.

"Oh, sit down!" said the old man. "And don't cry. I *hate* it when people cry." He stopped eating and lifted his face to stare, not at Elsa but at the far shore of the river. "I told you I know why you're here. In fact, I came to the bridge because I knew you'd come. I am Frau Gruber's husband, of course. You might have guessed."

"I looked for you because I am very worried about . . ." Elsa started to say.

"I know, I know," said the old man, waving her quiet. "Listen to me. I am going to tell you something quite strange. But first, you look small and frail to me. Are you able to hear shocking and terrible and curious things without crying and carrying on? I *hate* crying and carrying on."

"Yes," Elsa said.

"All right," said the old man. "First, the story about the devil and the sorcerer and Frau Gruber is true. My soul has been ransomed to the devil. Unless I can do something to break this spell, when I die I'll be, as we say, a dead goose."

"How could . . . ?" was all Elsa could say before the old man waved her quiet again.

"Second, Frau Gruber herself is a skillful sorceress. Do you want to know where your friends Klaus and Teresa are? I'll tell you where they are. Don't you think I know where they are?" He snorted and wiped a hand across his nose.

Elsa nodded.

"I have ways of knowing these things," he said, quite satisfied with himself. "She has sold their souls to the devil, just as she sold mine."

"Oh, how terrible!" cried Elsa, putting her hand to her mouth.

"There you go!" snapped the old man. "I asked you if you were strong enough to hear shocking and curious things. Are you going to cry and carry on now?"

"No," said Elsa, who was determined that she would show no weakness to this foul old man.

"I'll tell you something," he said, fixing Elsa with a stare from one of his red eyes. "Right now, your friends are wandering around somewhere, old and wrinkled and pained as I am, the soul and the juices sucked right out of them. Their skin is dried-up and lifeless and their teeth are bad and their fingers are dirty. They probably are eating scraps and living like animals. Sooner or later they may wish that some farmer would shoot them and put them out of their misery." The old man, Elsa noticed, seemed to enjoy describing scenes of wretchedness.

"What," she asked, "was Frau Gruber to gain by doing such a terrible thing?"

"Frau Gruber probably sold them to buy more time, more youth and, of course, more glory." The old man flipped another crust of food into his mouth. "Everyone seems to want youth and glory, you know." He paused a moment. "And it's not so amazing, her sorcery. In fact, I've learned a little magic myself. How do you think I knew you were coming to see me?"

"You know magic?" asked Elsa.

"Of course! Do you think all I do is sit on river-banks? Are you accusing me of being a lazy old man?"

"No," said Elsa.

"Well, I should think not. Now I want you to do something. Do you want to save your friends?"

"Oh, yes!" Elsa cried. "More than anything."

"Then take this with you." From deep in the folds of his dirty coat, the old man produced a crinkled and dirt-smeared piece of paper with a musical composition written on it. "At your next lesson, play this for Frau Gruber. You do play, don't you?"

"Yes," said Elsa, noticing that the music didn't look very difficult to play.

"Good, for it must be played note-for-note, leaving nothing out. When you are finished, come back and tell me everything that has happened."

When she returned to the orphanage, Elsa was punished for leaving without permission. Her punishment was to help Frau Hanfstangl wash dishes for a week.

At the next lesson, Elsa was very nervous, which made it difficult for her to sit silently while the other students played their lesson pieces. She looked several times at the grimy piece of paper from the old man. If Frau Gruber finds out, she thought to herself, she may turn me into a stone on the spot. To make matters worse, the dog, Otto, seemed to glare at her from his rug in the corner of the room.

When it was time for her to play, she was relieved to see that Frau Gruber was tired and not very mindful of the music Elsa placed on the piano. At the first notes of the piece, which appeared to be little more than a pleasant little waltz, Frau Gruber began to doze off to sleep. Remembering what the old man had said about playing it through carefully, note-for-note, Elsa continued to play, striking each note precisely until the last note had been played. By this time, Frau Gruber was snoring loudly with her head resting against the great Glueckmann piano.

Returning with the students to the orphanage, Elsa found Klaus and Teresa, looking tattered and dazed but otherwise quite normal, sitting on the steps. She was so happy she hugged them both.

"You wouldn't believe what happened to us," Klaus said, his eyes wide.

"I know," she said, her heart pounding. "And I have an amazing story to tell *you*. But now you must come with me to Frau Gruber's cottage."

They rushed back to the cottage as fast as they could run, and tiptoed to one of the windows. Taking great care not to be seen, they looked inside. There they saw Frau Gruber, looking older than she had ever been, racing about the music room, pulling at her ears, striking the piano keys and screaming at Otto, who didn't seem to hear her at all.

"No, no, no, no!" she screamed. "I hear nothing, NOTHING! I am DEAF AS A STONE! How can I hear the music?" She tore at her hair, pulling it from her head in great clumps. She tore at her dress and punched her hands against the walls until her fingers were bloodied and broken.

"Whoever has done this to me, I will tear their hearts out and roast their livers for my dinner!" she screamed. "A thousand curses on them!"

"Otto doesn't hear her," said Elsa. "They both have lost the ability to hear."

As they watched, Frau Gruber screamed at Otto again, then walked over and kicked him swiftly in the backside before throwing herself sobbing at the piano, smashing her face on the keys so hard that she knocked herself unconscious and fell in a heap on the floor. Startled, Otto leaped into the air and ran wildly across the room, knocking over a table near the door on which Frau Gruber's large kerosene lamp always sat. It fell to the floor and burst into a roaring wall of flame. Within seconds the entire cottage was engulfed in fire.

Backing away in terror, the children heard the plink! tink! twang! of breaking wires on the great Glueckmann piano as the wires succumbed to the intense heat.

Instead of returning to the orphanage, Elsa took her terrified friends by the hands and ran toward the country, to the tiny bridge where she had found the old man. When they reached the bridge, the old man was nowhere to be found.

"I don't understand," said Elsa, still shaking. "He promised to be here."

"A promise kept," said a much younger and fuller voice. From behind the bridge stepped a handsome, well-dressed man who was very clean and smelled faintly of lavender cologne. He was smiling as he held out his arms to hug all three children. "I spent many years searching for a means to break the spell and take back my soul from the devil," he said. "And you have helped me do so. Frau Gruber was willing to sell our souls for her music, so I took away her music. Now, with the fire, the devil *has* a soul, and it is Frau Gruber's."

"You're much younger than you . . . were," said Elsa when she finally regained her voice.

"Now that the spell is broken, I've regained a measure of my youth," he said gently.

"Perhaps you can come and visit us," said Elsa. "We must return to the orphanage or we'll be punished. I don't want to do any more dishes for Frau Hanfstangl."

The man kneeled down and put his face very close to the children's faces. "Permit me to make you an offer," he said, still smiling. "In learning music, I also learned how to find wealth. If the three of you would like to live with me in the country, you may do so. You may study music as much as you wish, in the finest schools. I will take a wife and we will live as a family, with no fear and no more evil sorcery."

Elsa and her friends were too overcome to speak.

"But again," said the man, "perhaps you would rather spend your days with Frau Hanfstangl and her soup . . ."

"We have dreamed of this for so long," Elsa finally said, her voice wavering.

"Then it is done," said the man, clasping his new family close to him.

COLOR CRAZY

A science museum, Greg decided, can be kind of an interesting place. Where else can you check the fingernails on a scary-looking 3,000-year-old mummy, get friendly with a dinosaur, and come face-to-face with a ten-foot stuffed grizzly bear, all in the same day?

For the past two hours, Greg and John, his friend from school, had been looking at whales' skeletons, checking a space-age television phone display, seeing the stars and planets on a dome-shaped screen, and looking at the weird ways ancient people and animals lived.

They nearly were thrown out of the museum when John decided to make burp noises in one display hall where the walls made great echoes. The guard only told them to settle down, though, and let them stay.

Later, while John went to find the boys' bathroom, Greg wandered about the central hall, looking at glass cases filled with stuffed birds, snakes, and things he'd never seen before. As he looked, he heard a man's voice talking into a microphone in a meeting room near the corridor. The room had a sign outside that said: "Color and the Way People Behave."

The guy speaking was old, with thick glasses down on his nose and stringy hair slicked flat on his head. He wore a bow tie that jumped a little every time he spoke.

"The way we act often depends on color," the man was saying. "That's why studios used for television news often are painted pastel blue, or other 'gentle' colors that help to relax viewers. Babies' rooms often are painted in gentle colors, too. That's also why schoolrooms are never, ever, painted in colors like bright red, which could make students more excited and harder to quiet down."

Greg had never thought of that. Come to think of it, though, the rooms in his school *were* painted in mostly whites and light blues and tans.

John found Greg leaning near the doorway to the lecture room. "Let's take off," he said. "I gotta get home."

"Okay, in a minute," whispered Greg. "I want to hear what this guy says about why colors make you happy or sad."

"Animals tend to be color-blind, while most humans

76

can tell one color from another," said the man. "Certain color combinations can affect people, too, making them feel more sad, or excited, or more mad. If somebody gets mad at you, it could be because of something you're wearing, or the color of the room you're sitting in. It's important to remember, though, that everyone is different, and what affects one person one way may not affect the next person at all . . ."

Weird, thought Greg. I wonder what colors our grumpy old neighbor, Mr. Cosgrove, can't stand. Seems like he's *always* threatening to punch somebody for one thing or another. And his dog's as mean as he is. Stupid Doberman always acts like it wants to take a piece out of me.

Later that evening, Greg looked around his house, trying to observe, for the first time, how colors were placed, and what the rooms were painted. Most of the rooms were painted beige. Hardly exciting.

"I put some stuff in the dryer for you," said Greg's mom. "There're some clean jeans, and here's the new shirt from Grandma. She said she found it in a little shop where they paint the designs by hand. No two designs are alike."

"Do you know that colors can make you more happy or sad?" said Greg.

"I didn't know that," said his mother. "But I do know that if you don't go to bed now, there'll be some red color on your report card, in the form of some failing grades."

He went to bed thinking of rainbows and other colorful things. And he wished he could find a color to paint the fence that would bug crazy old Cosgrove.

In the morning, Greg was in a great mood. He quickly pulled on his jeans and the new shirt from Grandma, stuffed some toast in his mouth and headed for the bus stop.

In school, his teacher, Miss Warner, seemed to have something on her mind. She didn't seem to smile, or even talk as much as usual.

"John and I went to the Science Museum yesterday," said Greg. "We saw everything from saber-toothed tigers to a ten-foot . . ."

He never got a chance to finish the sentence. "I haven't time to listen now, Greg," said Miss Warner. "You get to your work. You know the assignment."

Greg couldn't wait to get outside when lunchtime came. Students who finished their lunch early were allowed to go outside for a few minutes and use the playground equipment before coming in to begin the afternoon classes. Sometimes the guys even got in a short basketball game on the outdoor hoop before the bell rang.

He sprinted for the playground and looked around for some of the usual group. He was hoping one of them might have gotten out even before he did, and might have a ball to use. He headed for the hoop, but no one was there.

Oh, well, thought Greg, I'll sit on the swings a little

and maybe they'll show up. When he sat down on one of the swing seats, two girls who had been swinging jumped off the swings and ran away.

Greg thought it was strange that no one seemed to be hanging around the basketball court like usual, and especially strange that no one else was swinging. On most days, the swings were in constant movement, with kids swinging, jumping and climbing on the swing supports. Maybe there's an assembly going on or something that I don't know about, thought Greg.

While he sat on the swing, trying to remember what might be going on, he heard the sudden swoosh! of something flying through the air, and a rock clanged! off one of the steel swing supports.

"Hey!" yelled Greg. "Who's throwin' rocks?"

Before he finished speaking, another rock hit the top support.

"Hey!" he yelled again. "Knock off the rocks!"

At the far end of the playground, someone began yelling and pointing at Greg. Others joined in, and they began to walk toward him, pointing and yelling.

When they were closer, he noticed they were yelling just two words: "Get him! Get him!"

"What the heck does that mean?" Greg yelled to the advancing students. "What'd *I* do?"

"Get him! Get him!" yelled the group, which now had grown to more than a dozen, both boys and girls.

Another rock sailed through the air and hit the top

of the swing. "What the heck is the matter with you guys?" yelled Greg. "Are you crazy?"

"Kill! Kill!" shouted the group. More began to throw rocks. One bounced off the basketball hoop.

He began to panic and tried to sprint for the school door, but more kids blocked the way. He darted first one way and then another, trying to get around and outrun them. Everywhere he moved, however, there were kids, snarling and scowling at him.

"Get him! Get him!" yelled the students.

"No! Knock it off!" Greg screamed, holding one hand in front of his face. "I didn't do nothin'."

The attack stopped as quickly as it had begun. Those students nearest Greg began to smile and the chants stopped. His friend John stepped from behind the crowd. He was laughing.

"Surprise!" they shouted. "The joke's on you!"

"What's going on?" asked Greg, still holding one hand up.

"It's just a joke," laughed John. "I got these kids to go along with it. We weren't gonna hit you or nothin'."

"What's the big idea?" asked Greg, starting to get mad.

"Aw, I was just telling these guys about that lecture thing at the museum you were talking about. You know, about how colors change your feelings and stuff. Somebody thought it'd be a riot to pretend we went crazy over your new shirt and totally freaked out."

"It's a crummy joke, and it's not too funny," said Greg, still angry.

"We didn't mean nothin'," John said, looking a little sorry—but not *too* sorry. "Honest. We just had a little fun. Besides, your shirt's awesome, with all the bright colors and stuff. I got a real special shirt, too. My dad bought it from an old man when he was doing some business in the Yucatan, down in the bottom of Mexico. It's a special color he called 'Maya blue.' More'n a thousand years ago, ancient Mayan people used to make human sacrifices and offer the bodies to their gods."

"Sounds gross," Greg said.

"I read about it, and it's kinda neat," John said, smiling. "They'd smear paint of that same special blue color on the victims before they tore their hearts out. I can wear the shirt tomorrow, if you want me to, so you can see it."

By the end of the school day, Greg was feeling more relaxed about the whole thing, and even laughed a little when John told it all over again to several of the kids on the bus going home.

"Shoulda seen the look on his face," John said, laughing out loud. "We're all yelling, 'Get him, Get him,' and he's thinking he's dead meat."

When Greg told his mother about the joke, she

shook her head, but didn't seem too upset. "It's a shame John made you the object of his joke," she said. "But at least no one was hurt. He wants to keep you for a friend, so I'm sure he won't do it again."

As she spoke, the doorbell rang. "Hey, there he is," said Greg, peeking through the window near the front door. He could see John standing on the step, idly tossing and catching a soccer ball.

"Wanna kick it around a little?" said John as Greg opened the door.

"Yeah, I guess." Greg joined his friend in the yard and they began taking some shots at the front step, pretending it was a goal net.

Within minutes, Greg heard Mr. Cosgrove next door start his lawn mower. He could just barely see Mr. Cosgrove's reddish, scowling face as he moved back and forth across his lawn.

"Say hi to old Mr. Friendly," John said, grinning and nodding toward the neighbor. He gave the ball a hard shot that bounced off the step and spiraled over the fence—directly into Cosgrove's yard.

"Great," said Greg. They saw Mr. Cosgrove reach down and retrieve the ball, then look in their direction. He stopped his mower without taking his eyes off Greg. Staring intently, he walked to the fence and looked over. "Uhh . . . Hi," Greg said, as John snorted slightly and tried to muffle a laugh.

Silently, slowly, Mr. Cosgrove walked around the

end of the fence and took a couple of steps into Greg's yard. Somehow, Greg thought, the old man looked ridiculous standing there, his belly hanging out between frayed suspenders, trying to look threatening. Cosgrove stepped forward suddenly and grabbed Greg, lifting him upward with one arm. He pulled his other fist back, ready to strike.

"Hey!" Greg yelled, his smile fading.

"I'll call your ma out here," said John, bounding over the step toward the door.

"No, wait!" Greg said, waving his arm. He noticed that old Cosgrove's eyes were rolling back in his head and his mouth was sagging open. He already had lowered Greg back to the ground, and now was gripping his own chest with his other hand as he fell to one knee. "Tell Mom to call the paramedics," yelled Greg as Mr. Cosgrove flopped over onto his side on the grass. "He's having like some kinda heart attack or something!"

Through the window in the kitchen Greg saw his mother dialing and shouting their address into the phone. She slammed down the receiver and ran outside, calling to Greg as she ran. "Get a blanket," she said, "and get something for under his head." Within seconds, Greg could hear the distant sound of a siren.

As he turned to respond, he caught a blur of motion in the corner of his eye and a tremendous force bowled him over, knocking him flat on his back not far from

Mr. Cosgrove. Greg's mother screamed as Greg pushed at the slashing bared teeth and wriggling, muscular form of Cosgrove's Doberman as it lunged at his throat and head and arms.

Drops of Greg's blood spattered his face and neck. He held his arms up to try and protect himself from the dog's furious attack. An ambulance screeched to a stop at the curb and Greg heard neighbors and men from the ambulance shouting above the gurgling, snarling fury near his face. Greg's shirt and even part of his jeans were now ripped and bloody. From somewhere came several men's feet, kicking at the animal, which remained focused intently on Greg and the cloth in its mouth.

Finally, a strong boot knocked the animal aside and someone pulled Greg free while other neighbors pushed and poked at the dog with boards and rakes to keep it at bay.

"Police came and got the Dobie," said John, sitting with Greg's mother in the waiting room near the hospital emergency suite after Greg's wounds were stitched and he was bandaged. "The dog's in the pound, I heard. And I guess old Cosgrove's gonna make it."

"It's kinda weird," Greg said through a bandage on his lip as they walked slowly toward the hospital parking lot. His arms, chest, and face were covered with stiff, uncomfortable bandages. "You think Cosgrove and the dog attacked me because of that shirt I was wearing?"

"No, no, of course not," his mother said. "It seems like Mr. Cosgrove is always ready to hit someone. The dog just thought you'd hurt his master. Some dogs are very protective."

"Yeah, I know," John said. "Gimme a nice little lap dog anytime." He turned to Greg. "Hey, I'll bring your books home tomorrow, so you can keep up when you go back to school."

The next afternoon, John was in the schoolyard, chewing fast to get the gum in his mouth nice and soft so he could put it on the swing seat before the girls came out. He casually placed the wet, pink wad on the top of the seat, making sure he didn't get any on his new Maya blue shirt. Then he slowly sauntered away, trying to notice whether anyone sat in it.

Turning toward the basketball hoop, he was startled when a rock sailed past his face and hit the dirt behind him.

"Hey!" he yelled. "Gimme a break! Not so close!"

As he turned, he saw nearly a dozen boys and girls advancing on him, chanting, "Get 'im! Get 'im!"

"Right," John called out to the group, grinning. "Cute joke. Sorry it's been used." As he spoke, another rock sailed through the air, and this one hit him in the leg. The pain was sharp where the edge of the rock struck.

"Ow! Enough!" he yelled. "Some idiot hit me!"

Still they came, advancing in a solid line, chanting in rhythm. "Get 'im! Get 'im!"

"Sean!" John yelled, recognizing a familiar face. "It was funny yesterday with Greg, but this is pretty stupid. What the heck's the matter with you guys?"

"Get him!" screamed Sean, whipping another rock in John's direction.

John sprinted, as Greg had the day before, toward the school, but again the crowd blocked the way. Everywhere he moved, there were more kids.

Now in a near-panic, he began to scream for help from the school, but the chanting drowned out his voice. Slam! Another rock struck him in the stomach, doubling him over. When he was bent over, another rock struck him on the back of the neck, and he fell to his knees. The crowd's screams were deafening now, with students all around screeching at the tops of their voices.

The rocks were coming in a shower now. Someone kicked John hard, knocking him over on his side in the dirt. As he tried to stand up, several rocks struck him straight-on in the face. As he slammed backward onto the hard ground, a hand reached out and grabbed the front of his new shirt from the Yucatan. The last thing he saw through the blood and dust in his face was the strange, twisted face of his friend Sean, staring at the cloth in his hand, then Sean's fist smashing downward, toward his head.

FOREST EYES

"How much wood would a woodchuck chuck, if a woodchuck could chuck wood?" Tammy said again, boosting her sleeping bag into the back of Michelle's dad's station wagon. "I don't know where my dad got that."

"If you say that anymore," Michelle grumbled, "I'll stuff your mouth full of cheese popcorn and tape it shut."

"What does it mean to 'chuck wood'?" Tammy asked, smiling and making a face at Michelle.

"I dunno. I'm not a Girl Scout, and neither are you."

"Well, we should have a great time, anyway," said Tammy, who refused to be anything but cheerful. "How many girls are there? Eight or ten of us? And we've got the whole weekend to sit by a mountain campfire and sleep in tents and eat about eighty pounds of junk food. Sounds great to me."

"We'll all come back fat," said Michelle, pushing a picnic cooler into the back, beside more sleeping bags.

"It's nice of your sister, Jean, and Nicole's mom," Tammy said. "It was a great idea. I hope we can all fit in two cars. How far is it to the mountains?"

"I dunno. Two or three hours or something."

"Your sister," Tammy said, laughing a little and whispering at the same time. "Did you see those nature books she's taking? I think she figures we're gonna turn into Smokey the Bear."

"Yeah, she's really into outdoor stuff. She's studying forestry in college. She's always telling me what trees are called and what kind of things you can eat in the wild and how you could survive and things like that."

"Guess there's nothing wrong with that," said Tammy, poking around among the tents and bags to find gum. "Does she *really* think we need this much toilet paper?"

"Hey, Michelle!" Wendy called from the other car. "Look what Kimberly's taking." She held up an electric-orange, two-piece swimming suit."

"Gimme that!" Kimberly said, grabbing the suit. "Maybe we'll find a river or something."

"Yeah, fulla little things with pinchers on 'em," laughed Wendy.

An hour or so out of the city smog, a few of the

girls in both cars had settled back to sleep, while others idly watched the passing scenery turn from a few small towns to rolling desert to gradually higher and bushier mountain country.

Tammy, who always had trouble sleeping in cars, leaned back on the seat, pulled her cap down over her eyes and muttered, "How much wood would a woodchuck . . ."

Before she finished the sentence, Michelle's hand swung over and squished several kernels of cheese popcorn into her mouth.

"Mummphff!" coughed Tammy, then laughed out loud, pulling the cap down completely over Michelle's face and spilling popcorn over part of the floor in the back seat.

"Hey, you guys!" said Michelle's sister, in a way that meant "knock it off."

As Michelle curled up to sleep some more, Tammy picked up one of the books Jean had brought and began to read. When Michelle awoke later, Tammy was still reading.

"Listen to this," Tammy said. "It says, 'Though relatively small, the wolverine is exceptionally intelligent and fearless and takes on any opponent, even grizzly bears. Indians called him the forest devil. With powerful forepaws and slashing claws, he is extremely dangerous when cornered . . .' "

"I don't think I want to hear about those," said Michelle.

"That's nothing. Listen to this," Tammy continued. "This is about mountain lions. 'Although most are extremely timid, they should be treated with caution. There are a few recorded instances in which mountain lions killed and *ate* humans.' "

"Geez, Tammy!" Michelle said, her anger rising. "This is great stuff just before we go into the mountains."

"Oh, so what," Tammy said, waving her hand. Her face was still intently fixed on the book. "I never knew some of this stuff. Did you know some kinds of bats are more than seven inches long? It's got stuff on badgers and bears in here, too, and rattlesnakes, bobcats, and mountain king snakes . . ."

"Jean!" Michelle called out from the back seat. "Can you take that stupid book of yours and keep it up there? I want to be able to sleep tonight."

"Relax," Jean said. "Some animals prey on others for food. Been doing it for millions of years."

"It's not in here," said Tammy, putting down the book, "but I heard once about these horrible vampire bats that come at night and swoop down and suck your blood . . ."

"Jean . . . !"

After they parked and locked the cars near a ranger station, Nicole's mom led the way up a steep mountain trail, with Jean walking behind them. The air, rich with the scent of pine and juniper, seemed crisp and sharp. It carried a hint of a cold night ahead, too, with the wind picking up off the jagged, white-topped peaks they could see in the distance. Michelle was glad Jean had insisted she take hiking boots instead of the canvas sneakers she had intended to wear.

"Anybody gets tired," Nicole's mom called back over her shoulder, "let me know. We'll be an hour or so on foot, and I know these packs get a little heavy. We have to keep going, though, because it's almost sundown already."

"A little heavy?" puffed Nicole, walking directly behind her mom. "I feel like I'm carrying my dad's car in my pack."

After they had stopped twice to rest, several of the girls began to complain that their shoulders were hurting from the pack straps.

"If I have to," groaned Tammy, walking just behind Nicole's mom, "I'll even dump the junk food unless we stop pretty soon . . ." Shifting her pack, she suddenly paused and whispered, "Hey, look. I just saw the top of a head. Somebody's coming down the trail."

Cresting a small rise, they met a tall, well-built young man walking toward them. He had long, wavy hair and a tan, solid-looking face. He carried binoculars and had the familiar ranger's patch on his shirt.

"Hello, folks," he said, smiling. "Be a little careful up ahead. The trail gets narrow, and some of the canyons are pretty deep."

"He's cute," whispered Kimberly.

"For a grown-up," whispered Wendy, stifling a giggle.

"Thanks," said Nicole's mom. "We aren't going much farther. I'm already getting complaints from the troops."

"I'll stop by later and make sure everything's all right," said the man, smiling and continuing down the trail.

Finally they came to a small clearing at the edge of a stand of scrub pine. The ground in the center was scuffed flat where other hikers had camped. Although the clearing was mostly level, the surrounding mountainside dropped away on three sides in a series of jagged, rock-filled gulches.

"No sleepwalking," said Kimberly, looking toward a distant canyon floor.

"My brother sleepwalks," said Monica. "We'd have to tie him to the tent pole."

After the tents were pitched in a circle around the concrete fire ring in the ground, and Nicole's mom had a nice little fire going, they took out sodas, hot dogs, and marshmallows. Soon the only illumination was the flickering, dancing firelight reflected in each of their faces.

"Hey, what if we have to go?" asked Wendy.

"To the bathroom?" Jean said. "Right there." She pointed off to one side at a pair of tiny structures barely visible just inside the tree line.

"Pretty far away," Wendy said, squinting at the trees.

"So, shall we sing a few songs, or what?" asked Tammy, her mouth half full of marshmallow.

"Naw, let's tell stories," said Monica.

"Shh . . . wait a minute," said Jean. "I heard something."

"Hello again," said the young ranger, stepping from the night shadows into the firelight. "Just thought I'd stop by and make certain you're all settled in." Looking around, he smiled again. "I didn't mean to startle anybody."

"Uhh . . . no, that's fine," said Nicole's mom. "Care for a marshmallow?"

"Why not?" He sat down at the edge of the fire. "Try to stick pretty much to the trails tomorrow," he said. "Rattlesnakes have been known to come out midday and sun themselves on the rocks in some of these canyons."

"Wonderful," said Kimberly.

"We were about to tell some stories," said Nicole's mom. "Right, Monica?"

"Well," said Monica, "I just thought it'd be, you know, fun to tell scary stories around the campfire. Like, I read about this maniac once who killed and ate parts of people who were camping, and then slashed the bodies with mountain lion claws so people would think animals did it."

"Oh, gross, Monica!" Wendy said, shivering.

"Well, how do *we* know what's peeking at us from the forest when we pitch a camp?" said Monica, smiling.

"What a loonie," said Kimberly. "Maybe we should talk about something else."

"I think *Monica*'s the loonie," said Tammy, and everyone laughed.

"It's not unheard of," said the ranger, still laughing. "There *was* a young mountain man, kind of a recluse, around these mountains way back in the 1930s who used to attack campers at night, then hide the bodies. Probably the same guy you read about. He used to leave animal signs to confuse the searchers, and sometimes he ripped bodies with animals' claws attached to a special glove he wore. He was pretty clever. It took years before the disappearances were linked to the same man. But he was finally caught and executed."

"That's terrible!" said Nicole. "You sure they got him?"

"Oh, yes," laughed the ranger. "They got him, but it took a while. Well, I'm going to go now." He rose and started toward the tree line.

"Where the heck can you go at night?" asked Tammy, pausing in mid-bite.

"Oh, yes," said the ranger, turning and smiling again. "There's another ranger station over the rise a mile or so ahead, just beyond this stand of scrub pine."

"I'm glad to know it's there," said Nicole's mom, "especially after what we've been talking about."

"Ranger station or not," said Kimberly, after the

ranger was gone, "that stuff gave me the creeps."

"Me too," said Lisa.

"I got an idea," said Tammy. "What if there was a killer in the mountains, and he walked around dressed like a *ranger*, so nobody would suspect?"

"*Tammy!*" several girls squealed, throwing marshmallows at her.

"I think we've had enough for one evening," said Jean. "What do you say we all turn in?"

"Good idea!" said Kimberly. "If we stay out here any longer, I'm gonna throw Tammy into one of those canyons."

Within minutes, all the girls were settled into their tents, and Nicole's mom had scooped dirt and sand over the remaining embers of the fire. When the fire was gone, the surrounding mountain peaks took on a majestic beauty. Each was bathed in moonlight, with shadows covering the valleys like soft, black velvet.

Settled into the fluffy down of their sleeping bags, most of the girls were soon asleep. Although Michelle was very warm and comfortable, and the cool mountain air smelled wonderful, she still couldn't seem to get to sleep. She shifted and turned, this way and that, and finally managed to drift off.

When she awoke it was still dark outside, with the silhouettes of the mountains outlined, as before, against a moonlit sky. She pushed the little button on her watch and saw that she had slept only a few hours. At least an hour remained until daybreak.

"Darn!" she whispered to herself. "If I don't sleep, I'll be too pooped to carry a pack anywhere tomorrow." She raised herself up on one elbow to see if her friend Tammy was sleeping. Reaching to touch Tammy's sleeping bag, Michelle found it empty. That's strange, she thought. Pulling back the tent flap, she saw the dim outlines of the other tents in the moonlight. A cold night breeze gently stung her cheeks as she inched forward and stuck her head out of the tent.

The silence was eerie. From far below in one of the deep mountain canyons, she heard the short, bubbly warble of a bird, then silence.

When it came, the new sound startled her. Swish, swish, swish . . . It was the faint sound of grass being stepped on and crunched just beyond the tree line, near the outhouses.

Straining to see in the dim light, Michelle's heart nearly stopped. A figure of a man was walking slowly away from her along the edge of the woods beyond the clearing. In his arms he carried the limp figure of a girl. Her head bobbed slightly and her arms flopped a little as he walked.

Michelle opened her mouth, at first unable to make a sound, then screamed as loud as she could. Tearing open the tent flap, she jumped to her feet on the cold ground and screamed again, tearing at the flaps of the other tents as she did so, "Jean! There's someone out there! Oh, please! Jean!" she screamed, forgetting which tent was her sister's.

Within seconds, other girls were screaming and bolting from their tents, running around, trying in the dark to find the trail leading back down, away from the direction of the tree line.

Looking back, Michelle saw the man hesitate a moment. Then he lowered the girl he was carrying to the ground, jumped over her and ran after the screaming campers.

"Stop!" he commanded. He sprang toward the open space between the tents. The crunch of his boots drew quickly closer to the running girls.

Off to one side, Michelle heard the piercing scream of Kimberly, and several screams up ahead where other girls had run. Still running, she struck a large rock with her foot. She felt a sharp pain as her ankle twisted sideways, sending her spinning onto the hard ground.

The man's heavy boots slammed past her in the direction the other girls had run. "No! No!" Kimberly screamed. "Help me! Please help me! Oh, please!"

Michelle's heart was in her throat. She heard more screams, then the guttural sound of a man's voice farther down the trail.

"Girls! Stop!" This time the voices were those of Nicole's mom and Jean. "It's the ranger!" They swept the beams of their flashlights across the trail. "Come back! For your own safety, come back!"

One by one, still gasping from the fright and the run, the girls slowly walked back up to the campsite and sat down beside the fire ring.

"Help!" Kimberly screamed again from a distance. "I can't move!" As Nicole's mom and Jean pointed the beams of their flashlights in the direction of the voice, they saw only a hand flopping several yards away at the rim of a steep gulch.

Rushing to the edge, they saw Kimberly trying to free herself from gnarled tree roots just below the trail. "I fell down into here in the dark," she said, still pulling at her ankle. "I think I sprained it." The ranger appeared again out of the dark. Grabbing other roots sticking out of the bank, he swung down and lifted Kimberly out of the root tangle, then carried her back to the campsite.

The sun was now winking over the eastern peaks. "Looks like you and Kimberly were lucky," said Jean, gently probing Michelle's ankle. "No sprains. But you both better take it easy walking for a while." She turned to Tammy, lying against a tent with one arm over her eyes and forehead. "And you . . ."

"Yeah, I know," Tammy groaned. "My head still hurts. And my arm. Boy, my arm got scratched bad and it hurts."

"She must have run into something during the night and knocked herself out," said the ranger, turning to Nicole's mother and Jean. His eyes narrowed, ever so slightly. "I found her . . . and I was . . . bringing her back to you."

"If anybody wants to know," said Tammy, her arm still over her eyes, "I had to go to the bathroom during the night. After all that stupid killer talk, I decided to run like crazy to the outhouse and back. Something hit me hard. I guess the only thing it could have been was some stupid branch . . ."

Wendy and Monica suddenly laughed out loud, and soon everyone was laughing. "I think," said Nicole's mom, "we'll head back right away. We can get to the cars before noon and be home this afternoon."

As the girls began to pack their tents, the young man vanished into the tree line.

"I've never been so happy to see a station wagon in all my life," Michelle sighed three hours later, when the cars and the ranger station came into view. She tossed her pack with the others in a pile near the tailgate of her dad's wagon.

"Back so soon?" The ranger, a kindly-looking, gray-haired man stood near a green all-terrain truck with "United States Forestry Service" on the door.

"Oh, we had quite a night," said Nicole's mother, smiling wearily and dropping her pack near the tailgate. "Some of the girls mistook one of your rangers from the other station for a bogeyman. We had quite a panic in the dark for a while there."

"Heading home now?" said the man, smiling at the tired hikers.

"Yes!" said several girls at once. They flopped down on the ground and leaned back against the packs.

"Listen," he said, turning to Nicole's mom and Jean. "Could you spare a moment before you go? I need to check a couple things."

Michelle and Tammy tagged along as Jean and Nicole's mother followed the man up the steps into the station. From broad windows around one room, they could see for miles across a sweeping range of mountains.

The ranger sat on the edge of his desk and offered Michelle and Tammy a piece of candy from a nearby bowl. "This other ranger," he said. "Can you tell me what he looked like?"

"He was sorta cute," said Tammy before anyone else could speak. "Kinda young and tall, with wavy brown hair. He stopped by earlier last night, and we were all telling these scary stories and stuff, and he was telling about some guy back in the 1930s who killed and ripped people apart around here. Anyway, I got so freaked out, when I went to the bathroom during the night I ran fast and I guess I hit something and he found me. That's when *everybody* freaked out and ran around and went nuts."

"He was from our other station?" said the ranger, popping a candy into his mouth.

"Yes," said Jean. "We were maybe six or eight miles up the trail here, and without knowing it we ended up camping less than a mile from your other station."

"Psst!" said Jennifer and Lisa, peeking around the door into the office. "Psst! Tammy. Come out here." Tammy shrugged and walked outside as the ranger spoke.

"Couple hikers came through here a month or so

ago, and they'd seen him up there, too," the ranger said. He stood, took a book from a shelf behind him and flipped it open. "That's what bothered me. Did he look anything like this?"

"There he is with the wavy hair!" said Michelle, pointing at a black-and-white photo in the book. "What's this?" She flipped the book around to the outside cover, which read, "Annals of Crime."

"That picture was taken in 1934," the ranger said softly. "He was hanged that same year. One other thing: Our next nearest ranger station's more than twenty miles from here . . ."

"Michelle." Tammy stood in the doorway. She was shaking, and her face was drained of color. "You gotta see this." She stepped into the room and opened her palm. "The girls outside saw this stuck in the arm of the sweater I stuffed in my pack. I was wearing the same sweater last night . . ."

In the middle of her palm was a polished, needle-sharp claw, attached at its base to a torn strip of glove leather.

CHANGING BURT

Rick's grandpa had been in the tiny bookstore on Wabash Avenue in Chicago for as long as Rick could remember. Before Rick's grandpa had been born, his grandfather's father had owned it, and before that, *his* father had sold books to busy Chicago shoppers.

It was narrow, only a few feet wide, squeezed between a record shop and a sandwich counter, but it was deep, and the shelves rose high, more than two stories inside. It had a circular staircase, with a railing on the second floor and a rolling ladder on the ground floor to reach some of the higher shelves.

In the back, near the tiny office where Rick's grandpa did his bookwork and kept his papers, was a small closet. Somebody must have meant it to be used for coats long ago, but as long as Rick could remember, the closet always had been Burt's home. Burt was a big, lazy, floppy-eared, terribly good-natured basset hound with deep, moist, loving eyes and very little ambition at all.

Burt also was quite old, as dogs go, but since Rick's grandpa was old, too, they made a good pair. Watching them, Rick thought they seemed more like two old well-matched friends than dog and owner.

Each day at noon, Rick's grandpa snapped a worn leash on Burt's collar, locked the front door to the bookstore, and took Burt for a walk for an hour or so to a park that wasn't very far away.

Even in the winter, when the terrible, bitter winds came screaming off Lake Michigan, they still went for a walk each day. They just didn't go so far in winter. When it was really cold, Rick's grandpa put a little knit wool cover on Burt. In summer, Rick's grandpa took a sandwich each day in a paper bag and had a nice lunch in the park with his friend Burt.

At night, the old man snapped the leash on again and took Burt home with him to his apartment not far away, where the landlord bent the rules a little and let a few people keep pets.

Rick and his best friend, Tony, liked to take the elevated train from Evanston, the Chicago suburb where they both lived, downtown to visit the bookstore whenever they could. Rick's grandpa always had

103

a large jar of English toffee and lemon drops on the little desk in his office, and he didn't mind if the boys ate them. They sometimes carried out trash, dusted books, and ran errands in return.

He also let the boys browse among the books and look at interesting ones, as long as they were very careful not to tear delicate pages or bend the bindings.

Since Rick's grandpa sold mostly used and hard-to-find books, some of the volumes were very strange. Some were very, very old books that had been purchased from libraries and collections in Europe and other parts of the world.

Sometimes they even found old, leather-bound volumes on subjects like witchcraft and sorcery and spells. The boys liked those the best.

What they *didn't* like to do, however, was visit the shop when Mr. Belness was there. Mr. Belness was a heavy, perpetually sweating man with thin hair, who wore expensive silk business suits and flashy jewelry. He always had a heavy gold ring with a blinding white diamond set in it on each little finger and a heavy gold-nugget wristwatch and massive gold cuff links. Sometimes even his shoes had little gold chains on the tops.

Every time he came to the bookstore—and that was more and more often—Mr. Belness and Rick's grandpa argued over the business. Mr. Belness had bought the little sandwich shop next door and the record shop on the other side. He also owned several other shops in the block. He was determined to buy all the shops in the block, tear them out, and build a hotel.

"I can pay you more than this old shop is worth and you can retire," Mr. Belness always said. "A man your age should be relaxing in Florida, on the beach. This is your golden opportunity."

"My father's father was here, my father was here, and *I'm* here," Rick's grandpa said more than once, his voice rising. "Since my wife passed away, this shop, and Burt, and my sons and my grandchildren are all I have—and they're all *here*. So why would I want to be in Florida? You don't talk sense."

"I'll get this property anyway, sooner or later," Mr. Belness always said. "You can't stop progress. Besides, it's a firetrap. One little match and you're all done."

Rick's grandpa was always upset for a long time after Mr. Belness left. He would go around among the books, arranging and rearranging them and muttering to himself. "Such a big shot, this Belness," he would mutter. "So you tear everything out and you build another big, fancy hotel. This is progress?"

"Belness is such a jerk," Rick said to his grandpa one day as Rick and Tony sat in the little office petting Burt and eating toffee.

"He's not the only jerk," Rick's grandpa said, pulling slowly on his large, silver-colored moustache. "Where I live, the building manager just retired. Now I have to deal with a younger fellow and he says, 'No pets.' "

105

"What the heck will you do with Burt?" said Rick. He gave Burt a scratch behind the ear. Burt moved his tail slightly at the sound of his name.

"I guess for now he stays here." Rick's grandpa stared a moment at Burt, half-asleep beside Rick's chair. "Maybe it's not so bad," he said. "He can be the watchdog when the store is closed."

Rick and Tony smiled.

"Slurp," licked Burt, rolling his tongue in a broad arc across Rick's fingers. His tail flicked once, then again.

"Burt's basically a one-flick dog," said Tony. "If he's happy, he flicks his tail once. If he really likes you, you might get two flicks. No more."

The next time the boys were in the shop, they found some more very old books on ancient magic, and a dusty volume on medieval history.

"Listen here," Tony said, leafing carefully through the pages. "People long ago thought they could turn lead into gold."

"Alchemists," Rick's grandpa said. "But it never worked. If it had, the world would be full of gold. People like Belness would be crazy with joy."

"Check this out," Rick said, slowly lifting a brittle page on a leather-bound book of "magik," which is how it was spelled on the book. "They got spells for everything in here." The pages smelled faintly of mildew, and many of the words had strange spellings.

He laid the book carefully on his grandfather's desk

and began to read aloud as Tony looked over his shoulder. "Lamb's blood, eye of newt, soil of the earth . . ."

"What the heck's a newt?" Tony asked.

"A salamander," said Rick's grandpa. "Lizard. Some people long ago thought some lizards had special powers, and could live in fire."

"Wow . . ." said Tony, staring again at the old book.

"It's not for nothing that I worked around books this long," said the old man, rising to go and greet a customer at the front of the shop.

"This is awesome," Rick said, still absorbed in the volume. "They got stuff in here about how much, and you gotta mix stuff when the moon is right, and you gotta sprinkle this and that . . . here it says, 'bone of fresh-killed stag' . . ."

"Stag's a deer," Tony said. "I know that much."

"Hey, my uncle Bill's got a market, right?" said Rick, closing the old book.

"Yeah. So what?"

"So he gets meat someplace. I bet he knows a place where they get lamb chops ready for market, and maybe even deer bones."

"I still don't get it," said Tony. "What ya tryin' to do, whip up a magic potion?"

"Why not?" Rick said, smiling. "Let's see what happens."

"Nothin', that's what happens," said Tony. "That

sounds like a lot of foolin' around to get dumb stuff like a drop of lamb's blood. Geez, not to mention a lizard. And what are you gonna do? Change yourself into Superman?"

"Naw. I just want to mess around with a recipe or two. Just for fun."

The next time they were in the shop, Tony already had forgotten about the magic, and instead became absorbed in a fascinating volume on prehistoric hunters and the game they hunted.

"Imagine taking on a mean old cave bear with a stone-headed spear," he said, showing Rick drawings of weapon-wielding cave men. "Oh, wow!" he said, flipping the page. "Look at this! He's one mean dude." The book carried a detailed sketch of a saber-toothed cat tearing great chunks of flesh out of the body of a prehistoric camel. The cat in the picture had a short tail, long, razor claws, a massive head with diamond-sharp glittering eyes and powerful, rippling shoulder and neck muscles.

The picture riveted Rick's attention as Tony read aloud. "Often four feet high at the shoulder, these animals had enormous saw-edged teeth, as long as five or six inches, with which they stabbed and slashed their victims. The victims included even elephants and rhinoceroses."

"Gee," Rick said, "can you imagine meeting one of those guys and he's hungry and *you're* supper?"

Both boys shivered at the thought.

"Hey, look," said Rick, turning from the book and producing a small plastic bag he'd brought from home. "Check it out."

Tony put down the cat picture and peeked inside. The bag held several smaller plastic bags, all taped shut. "Yeah?" he said. "So what's in the little bags?"

"I found this dead salamander and his head's in there," said Rick. "This one's got a little lamb's blood from Uncle Bill's market, and he found a deer bone for me. There's a little piece of it in there. This one's got plain old dirt, or 'earth,' the way the magic book put it, and . . ."

Tony laughed out loud. *"That's* what this is all about? You're back with that magic junk? Why don't you just learn a few card tricks and forget this messy stuff?"

"Let's try it," said Rick, smiling. "What can it hurt? Besides, we got teachers' convention tomorrow and Friday, so we got no school and nothing to do. You got a better idea?"

"So what do we do with this potion?" Tony asked.

"How should *I* know?"

"Let's try it on old Burt," said Tony. "Anyway, he can eat all that crud and it won't hurt him whether the magic works or not."

"Okay, let's do a spell and turn him into something."

"Yeah, but what?"

"Maybe your saber-toothed cat, there. But only for a little while. I'll sneak the picture of the cat over by where Burt sleeps. Spell's supposed to work best if you have an 'image' of what it is you're tryin' to make him into."

"Right," Tony said, laughing. "After that, we'll whip up some wings for ourselves and cruise on out to Hawaii."

Watching to make sure Rick's grandpa didn't see, the boys quickly pulled the old, leather-bound book off the shelf and turned to the page Rick had found before. They mixed the items Rick brought from home into a small plastic cup. Then they poured the mixture into Burt's water dish.

"School's out, so we'll stop by tomorrow," said Rick when his grandpa returned.

"Nice," said the old man. "Bring a sandwich. You can eat lunch with Burt and me in the park. Maybe we can get an ice cream after."

"Full moon tonight," said Rick on the train home. "I'm gonna go out in our yard and say some of the words they've got in the book. I copied 'em down."

"You gotta be kidding," said Tony. He smiled. "Yeah, I know. What does it hurt?"

The next morning, the boys arrived at the shop to find two police cars outside. A man with a camera and two policemen with plastic cases were just walking out the front door.

"We'll do what we can, but at this point, I'm not sure what to tell you," one policeman was telling Rick's grandpa. "Obviously something terrible happened in there, but we still can't be certain what."

The boys followed Rick's grandpa to the office at the back of the shop, and there they found a shocking scene. Books were scattered all about, furniture was smashed, papers were all over and blood was splashed all over the walls and floor.

"It's the work of a maniac, a madman," said Rick's grandpa. "Vandals. That must be it. Or druggies. And the police found matches and a can of lighter fluid, too. But no bodies."

"What about Burt?" Tony asked.

"Some watchdog," said Rick's grandpa. "Some vicious animal I got here." He looked down as Burt wandered past the desk.

"I'm glad they didn't hurt him," said Rick, gently stroking Burt's head as he came near. "Hey, listen! He's breathing real weird!" Burt's mouth was open wide, and from it came a high-pitched wheeze.

Burt twitched and his head flopped up, then back down. His head jerked and he flipped up again, almost losing his balance.

"Gaack," said Burt, lurching toward his closet. "Gaack, kaak!" His middle was heaving and he was shaking.

"He's choking!" shouted Tony. "He got somethin' caught in his throat. You gotta get that out."

"Here, Burt," said Rick's grandpa, trying to get hold of the dog. Burt lurched away again.

"Gaawwkk," gagged Burt, almost inside his closet

home. Then he coughed, and the wheezing abruptly stopped.

"Poor old buddy," said Tony, rushing to kneel down beside his four-footed friend, who was breathing normally again. Burt reached up and licked Tony's cheek. Putting an arm around Burt, Tony gasped. "Rick! Rick!" he whispered. "Oh, man . . ."

Rick and his grandpa hurried to the closet door and looked inside. On the floor in front of Burt was a fat little finger and part of a hand. On the finger was a massive gold pinkie ring with a huge, blinding diamond in the center.